Most
Valuable
Player

Most
Valuable Player

W. L. Heath

Illustrated by Spencer Lawrence

New York

Harcourt Brace Jovanovich, Inc.

ISBN 0-15-255720-2
Library of Congress Catalog Card Number: 72-88168

Printed in the United States of America
First edition
B C D E F G H I J

To my three halfbacks—
Cary, Warne, and Merrill—
who love the game of football and
have been pretty good hitters

Most Valuable Player

1

The coach was talking. We were all dressed and taped and ready, sitting around the locker room in that special atmosphere of tension that develops right before a game. This was supposed to be an easy one tonight—a breather before the big game with Baxter next week that climaxed the season—but the tension was there just the same. Through the window above Billy Foxx's head I could see one of the big banks of floodlights that lit the stadium, and I could hear the crowd noises and the sound of punting, which meant the Greensboro team was already on the field.

"Now, these boys don't have a lot of size," the coach was saying, "and their record, at five and three, is nothing much to brag about. But they are fast and they give it a lot of effort. Also keep in mind that there's nobody they'd rather beat than Morgan County High. It would be quite a feather in their cap. What I'm trying to impress on you is that a second-rate effort on our part is not going to take home the marbles. We've got to play football. You all know we've been pointing toward Baxter in most of our recent practice sessions, but tonight I want you to forget Baxter. Tonight we're playing Greensboro."

Our coach's name is Chip Stallings. He's a gray-haired man in his late forties now, but in his day he was quite a football player himself. You may even recognize the name. Chip was an all-American halfback at Virginia twenty-five years ago—one of the all-time great "climax" runners. If you follow football, you know what a climax runner is: he's the guy they feed the ball to in the clutch—the guy that can do magic for twenty, thirty, or maybe even ninety yards when the biggest fullback on earth can't make a nickel. Breakaway runners, they sometimes call them.

But while I was sitting there listening to him talk, I was thinking how one November afternoon twenty-nine years ago he had sat in a dressing room just like this one and heard another coach say the same sort of things he was saying now. You see, Chip Stallings wasn't only an all-American at Virginia, he was also the greatest player Morgan County ever had. This was his own high school alma mater, his own beginning place. He played his last high school game against Baxter—just as I was going to do, a week from tonight—and after that game they voted him Most Valuable Player. They gave him a gold cup, which still stands on the mantel in his living room, right in the middle of all his other trophies. I know about this because Chip Stallings is my father.

The noises coming from the stadium got louder. Somebody was thumping on a drum, cowbells were clanking, and now and then there'd be a ragged cheer—girls' voices mostly. I thought of Patsy Lloyd out there, leading the cheers, and I felt a little better—but only a little. Pat was still my gal, but just about everything else had gone wrong for me in the past month and half, and now with the Baxter game just one week away, my troubles had piled up to where I could hardly see over them. "Stay loose," Dad kept telling me. I was about as loose as a steel trap.

"Pete!" It was Dad, talking straight at me this time. "Pay attention to what I'm saying."

"Yes, sir. Sorry, Coach." Where football was concerned, he was the coach, not my father.

He had dragged a blackboard out in front of us, and now he began to diagram a play—one of theirs, not ours.

"This is something Greensboro put in especially for us," he said, "and it can hurt us if we don't stay alert."

The play was one of those cranky things a weak team will try sometimes in the hope of surprising a more powerful opponent: a pass thrown from a reverse. Greensboro had a left-handed boy playing right end who, according to our assistant coach Bob Dale, could chuck the ball a country mile. They'd start the play to the right, hand off to this guy coming back to the left, and then just when you had it figured for an end around, he would uncork a bomb to the flanker running a deep post. The important thing in defensing it was not to get sucked in and let that flanker get behind you—"you" being me, since I usually played deep safety on defense. "OK," I said to myself, "if that's all we have to worry about, Greensboro won't give us any trouble. I may even catch that one myself—outshine Billy Foxx for a change."

"One thing more," Dad said. "As all of you know, the triple option has been our bread-and-butter play for most of the season, but tonight we won't be using it."

I saw Billy Foxx's head snap up at that. The option was his big play, the one we'd used all year to spring him on those dazzling broken-field sprints he was famous for. I'd fake to the fullback, then go down the line to the right with Foxx behind me and trailing slightly. Depending on how their end played it, I'd either keep the ball myself or pitch it back to Foxx. Usually it went to Foxx.

"Let me qualify that," Dad continued. "We won't use it unless we have to. Is that clear, Pete?"

I nodded and pretended to frown, but actually I was enjoying that disappointed look on Foxx's pretty baby face.

"The reason I don't want to use it should be obvious enough. There'll be several Baxter scouts in the stands tonight, and there's no point in showing them our hand. We'll go with about five basic plays and hope that's all we'll need to beat these boys."

He pushed the blackboard away, dusted the chalk off his hands, and grinned at us. "All right, gang. Let's go out there and see if we can break a sweat."

There was a rousing shout as we grabbed our helmets and scrambled to our feet. We trotted out through the doorway and down the chute, cleats clattering on the concrete. As we went through the gate and onto the field, a tremendous roar went up from the seats, everyone yelling for Billy Foxx. "Foxx the fox," they called him. I heard it in my sleep.

"Sure," I thought, "cheer for Foxx, you stupid fans. Forget the rest of the team. Cheer for the great glamour boy."

12

I guess it's obvious by now that Billy Foxx wasn't exactly my favorite guy. And it all goes back to Dad and that gold cup on our mantel.

You see, my dad loves football the way some men love horses or airplanes or playing golf. It's been his whole life, either playing the game or coaching it. And so it was only natural, when I came along, that he started right in to make me the kind of player he'd been. As things turned out, I'm an only child; and I've heard Mom say that if I'd been a girl, she believes Dad would have jumped right out the hospital window the day I arrived. As a baby the first toy I ever had to play with was the little gold football on Dad's watch chain.

Maybe you're wondering why Dad was only a high school coach instead of a big college or pro one. He could have been, with his record. I asked him about it myself one time.

"What I like most about football is the spirit of it, Pete," he said, "and the way it develops boys into men. By the time you get to college, most of that is over and gone. It's more of a business than a sport. Same with the pros, only more so. High school football is where you find it—where you see it happening and have a chance to help it along. You know something? In many ways I'm prouder of that cup they gave me at Morgan than I am of making all-American." He really meant it, too.

Anyway, Dad started right in to make me a great player like himself. There's a word for it—vicarious, I think it is. He wanted to live the whole thing over again, through me. I've never blamed him for it, and I love the game myself; but at the same time it put me under a lot of pressure, trying to live up to his expectations. You might think a guy is lucky to have his own father for a coach, and maybe I am; yet there're some drawbacks to it. For instance, it's not enough for me to play well—I have to play perfectly. He never bawls me out when I make a mistake—Dad's not that kind of coach—but I can see the disappointment in his face, and somehow that hurts worse than getting flapped at.

He taught me to pass, to kick, and to run, long before I was out of junior high. Year after year he kept working with me—not pushing me to the place where I got frustrated or turned off, but just nudging me constantly along, polishing the rough spots. Many times after a workout in the backyard we'd go in the house, and if he was pleased with how I was doing, he'd point to that cup on the mantel and say, "Pete, one day there'll be two of those cups up there, just alike. That's a day I'm looking forward to."

Sometimes I think it worried Mom a little—she's the cautious, level-headed type. "Don't put too much emphasis on one thing," she'd say, meaning that one trophy. "After all, life is full of surprises and disappointments. Pete could get injured and not even play his senior year. Or somebody else might come along who just happened to be a better player."

"Who?" Dad would say, and laugh at her.

My sophomore year in high school I went out for the varsity and managed to play enough at back-up quarterback to earn a letter. I was pretty light that year and awfully young, and to tell you the truth, I don't think I was much good, though I did throw a couple of touchdown

14

passes before the season was over. I'll never forget the first game that year. We played Fairbanks High, and they beat us on a fumble that was my own fault—a bad hand-off. I felt terrible about it, but when the game was over, Dad gave me a reassuring pat on the back. "You played fine, Pete. Everybody fumbles now and then; don't let it get you down. You played hard and clean, and that's the main thing."

The next year I had gained twelve pounds, and for six games I was the hottest thing you ever saw. I was running the roll-out like Mister Cool himself, and if I threw a pass with my eyes shut, it fell in somebody's face for a TD. I was lucky. For a while it looked as though I was going to set that gold cup on the mantel a year ahead of schedule.

But then came a bad break. In dummy scrimmage one afternoon I turned my ankle so badly that I was out for the rest of the season. The thing just wouldn't get well. A boy named Stu Wallace won the cup that year playing at guard, with Dad casting the deciding vote—for Stu instead of me.

That brings us up to this year. And, brother, if I thought my luck went rotten last year, I had a book to learn.

To begin with, I was still gaining weight. The ankle was OK, but I was up to 180. That's not big for high school ball nowadays; but for me, standing only five feet nine, it was too much. I looked more like a middle guard than a quarterback, and it had slowed me down plenty. The roll-out stopped working for me because I was taking too long to get out there, running too long in the same place, as Coach Dale put it. And I couldn't seem to shed a pound, no matter how hard I worked.

But let's face it, my real headache wasn't the added weight. It was a guy named Billy Foxx, who had moved to town that summer. Foxx was a tall, slim, blond-haired kid who had never played a football game in his life. In fact, he had this sort of baby face. The girls all thought he was handsome, but he sure didn't look like any football player to me. That's another book I had to learn.

From the start he seemed to take a liking to me, and to be honest about it, I didn't think he was such a bad guy either, at first. He didn't know any other kids in town, and just because I was nice to him and friendly toward him, he took to hanging around me. His parents were divorced, and he lived with his mother, who had come to town to get work as a forelady at the hosiery mill. I guess I felt a little sorry for him. They didn't have much money, you could tell, because he wore the same clothes a lot and used to rake leaves and cut grass and stuff for his pocket money.

One day he said to me, "Pete, I'd like to go out for the team." We had just started pre-season workouts. "You think I could play football?"

I didn't think he could, but you don't put a guy down like that, so I said sure, come on out and give it a try.

"You know how it is with me and my mom," he said. "College is pretty much out of the question; but I was thinking maybe if I was good enough at something like football, maybe I could get a scholarship."

That really flattened me. Here was a guy that probably never had a football in his hands, the physique of a track man, and in one year of high school football he thought he had a chance of getting a college offer.

OK, what the heck. "Sure," I said. "Come on down to-

16

morrow and get dressed out. I'll give you a hand, help you all I can."

Good old bighearted Pete Stallings. I helped him all right. I must have helped him too much. Billy Foxx not only made the squad, he also made the lineup at tailback.

It was fantastic the way he developed. There's no other word to describe it. The guy was a natural. He was shifty, he was fast, and he had the best instinctive judgment of any broken-field runner I ever saw. But most of all, from the minute he first stepped on the field, the crowd loved him— he had flash. If I made seven yards, they cheered; if Billy Foxx made seven, they went wild. He made it *look* good . . . don't ask me how . . .

We lost our first game 28 to 21, but Billy Foxx made all three of our touchdowns, and he made them from beyond the thirty-yard stripe. I think I piled up more total yardage than he did, either running or passing, but it was his that paid off: a thirty-eight-yard pass interception, a forty-yard off-tackle waltz, and a fifty-nine-yard punt return that sent the crowd into hysterics.

We won our next seven games without any trouble, and by the time we came to Greensboro, Billy Foxx had scored so many touchdowns that people were saying he might even set a new school record. The old one, incidentally, belonged to my dad and had stood for twenty-nine years.

I should have been proud of him and happy for the team —and at first I was. But after a while it began to stick in my craw. The guy was driving me out of my tree, and that gold cup was getting harder and harder to see on my mantel. Not only that, he was starting to get the big head. He was beginning to think of himself as a star, which was something I just couldn't stomach.

"I think you're crazy," Patsy said to me when I happened to mention this to her one night. "Billy Foxx hasn't changed a speck; it's you that's acting dopey lately."

"Yeah? Then why has he started avoiding me? He used to wait for me every day after practice, and I'd give him a ride home. Now he acts like he hardly knows me."

"Maybe it's because you're turning into such an old grouch."

Maybe it was, but I had my reasons. I wasn't blind, either. Patsy, like all the other girls, was getting a little dazzled by Wonder Boy.

How was Dad taking all this? You'd have to know my dad to understand—I think he was sort of bewildered, really, sort of split down the middle. I know he hated to see me shoved out of the limelight by another player, yet he was too square a guy not to give Billy room to swing. As a matter of fact, he praised him, encouraged him, and even worked up some new plays that featured Billy. The triple option was one of them. The team always came first with Dad, and if that had meant putting me on the bench, that's exactly where he'd have put me, much as he might hate to do it. I guess I could sum it up by saying that Morgan High was having a great season and Dad was happy about that; but it was getting pretty gloomy around our supper table at night. And he had completely stopped talking about the Most Valuable Player award.

That's where things stood when we lined up for the kickoff against Greensboro . . .

2

Did I say this was supposed to be a breather? Excuse me. Halftime score: Greensboro 14, Morgan County zip.

It went something like this:

The opening kickoff fell to Dave Stone, our big fullback; and Dave Stone—who was an all-state basketball player and had not dropped a ball of any description within living memory—lost the ball in the lights. He not only fumbled it, he couldn't even *find* it afterward in the grass. If it hadn't been so serious, I guess it would have been funny—old Dave out there doing an Easter egg hunt while the ball rolled around behind him and in between his feet. Finally Skate Baker came over to help him look for it, but by that time they were swarmed under by green jerseys, and when the referee got them unstacked, Greensboro owned the football—at the nine.

Three plays later we were lining up for the second kick-off. The game was less than two minutes old and we were behind by seven points. You might say we were a little stunned.

This time the kick came to Billy Foxx, and he almost broke it all the way, going down the sideline to their seventeen or eighteen before being bumped out of bounds. I didn't like how easy they bumped him out—he should have bowed his neck and gotten another five yards—but the crowd of course went out of its mind.

On the next play—actually our first play from scrimmage—I called a little swing pass to the flanker, and threw the ball right in the hands of somebody wearing a green shirt. Jack Teas, the boy the pass was intended for, finally managed to catch him and haul him down; but it was their ball again, just over the fifty. I was almost afraid to look at our bench, but out of the corner of my eye I could see Dad and Coach Dale pacing back and forth past each other like a couple of switch engines in overcoats.

We held them without much trouble through the next series of downs—in fact, throughout the rest of the first quarter—but our offense just wouldn't jell. These boys from Greensboro had come to play ball, all right, and that quick seven-point edge had them fired up.

Each time we huddled, I could see Billy Foxx looking at me through his face guard, silently asking me to call the option; but I had my orders on that—orders I was glad to abide by. Let him stew, I thought. Let him look bad with the rest of us for a change.

We swapped the ball for a while between the thirties, and then finally, late in the second quarter, we got it going a little and worked it down to their fifteen by just running straight at them. It was the belly series mostly, with Dave Stone trying to redeem himself for that kickoff fumble. He was smacking that line like a freight train.

But then, wonder of wonders, just when we had a drive going, who should fumble the football but the great tailback himself. Billy Foxx coughed it up on a jarring tackle right over the middle. The ball went about twelve feet high in the air and came down in the hands of what must have been the fastest man in Green County. For a minute I thought I had an angle on him, but he blew right by me. He even out-ran Skate and Teas.

The point was good, and they led 14 to 0.

They led by more than that because now they were *really* up and we were down. They smelled an upset in the making.

What I smelled was rain. And sure enough, just as the horn sounded to end the half, a cold, dismal November rain began falling.

If you've ever played ball, you know what a dressing room is like at the half—steamy, sweaty, full of noise and chatter. If you're ahead, the noise has a happy sound; if you're behind, it's mostly grunts and groans and cusses. Dad was dragging his blackboard out again. It must have been 85 degrees in there, and he hadn't even remembered to take off his overcoat.

"Boys, we're beating ourselves," he said. "We're not playing football."

I expected he was going to tell me to start using the option, but instead he chalked up three plays, all three of which were passes. For a minute I thought he had flipped. Didn't he realize it was raining?

"I know it's raining," he said, apparently having read my mind, "but we're fourteen points down and we've got no choice about it—we've got to put the ball in the air. There's a good chance the pass will work now, too. We've been running at them for two quarters, and their half-backs are playing closer and closer to the line. Pete?"

"Yes, sir."

"I'm going to call some of the plays from the bench this half, so you'll have Edmonds at flanker a good part of the time. Keep that in mind."

I nodded. He alternated Edmonds with Teas to bring signals in from the side, and he didn't want me to forget which boy I had out there at any given moment of the game. Mel Edmonds was a gutty little player but very small, and he was weak on anything that called for a crackback block on the rover.

"We'll come out throwing the ball," Dad continued, "but that doesn't mean every play has to be a pass. Mix in your slants and sweeps, and also you might want to try the draw if they start shooting their linebackers."

"What about the triple option, Coach?" This was you-know-who talking. "Don't you think it's time we went to it?"

"Not quite yet, Billy. Let's play them one more quarter and then take another look at our hand. I still think we can beat these boys without it if we hustle. They softened up quite a bit toward the end of the half. I feel the score should be seven to seven right now; but of course they've had all the breaks."

That ought to shut him up, I thought. It was his big boo-boo that had put us in the spot we were in.

Dad talked on for a minute or two, then turned it over to

22

Coach Dale, who began to point out some individual things we were doing wrong—such as the guards weren't picking up the stunts, and the right-side linebacker was watching their quarterback instead of keying the guard.

I really wasn't listening anymore. I was thinking about something Dad had said: "You might want to try the draw." Actually, we had two draw plays—one where I handed the ball to Foxx, and one where I simply took a couple of steps back, faked the pass, and then went up the middle with the ball myself. I knew well enough which play Dad had in mind when he said "draw"—he was thinking of the tailback draw.

But he hadn't said so, had he?

We kicked off to them to start the second half (incidentally, I do the kickoffs, though Skate kicks the extra points), and it was raining hard enough to hear it hitting your helmet. I made the tackle myself at about the twenty—a good, hard shot that brought the fans out from under their umbrellas with a roar of satisfaction. There's nothing like making a clean, solid, open-field tackle to put you in the mood to play football. It looks good, it sounds good, it feels good. It starts the old Adrenalin flowing.

Three plays later Greensboro was still at the twenty, so they punted. It was a bad kick, going off the side of the kicker's foot and out of bounds at the thirty-five. We were in business.

Just then in comes Mel Edmonds, breathing hard with excitement because this is his first play, his first time in the game.

"What does he say, Mel?"

"Right, Formation One, Pass Three, X Circle!"

No wonder he was excited. On that play he was the primary receiver himself. I didn't like it much because it's not a good idea to ask a guy to catch a pass on his first play in the game. He's too keyed up. But Skate, the tight end, was my secondary target on this one, so just to play it safe, I dumped it off to him, and Skate broke it along the side for a brand-new first down at their twenty-two.

Let me take a minute here to tell you about Skate Baker. He's the only black guy in our starting lineup, and not only a great player but also a good influence on the team. Skate's strictly an up-beat type, always joking, always laughing, always optimistic. He's got the Afro haircut, the jive talk, and the fancy threads. He comes on like a one-man band, snapping his fingers, humming, and . . . I don't know, just being Skate. (The bane of Coach Dale's existence.) I happen to know privately that life hasn't been all that much fun for Skate, but you'd never guess it to be around him. It's just his personality. He bugs you sometimes, but he's irresistible.

"Man, did you see the jive move I put on that rover? I faked him out of his socks!"

He also talks too much in the huddle, but again that's Skate. Just when you're beginning to wonder if he's *all* talk, he hands you something like a first down at the twenty-two.

"Left, Formation One, Thirty-Seven Lead," I said. "First hike."

On this one Foxx gets the ball, running off-tackle on the weak side.

Foxx made eighteen yards after being checked at the line, and I have to say it was a beautiful thing.

Anyway, we were camped at their four, and the second half had barely started. This is the kind of football we were supposed to play.

I looked over toward the bench and saw Dad walking along the sideline in the rain with his arm looped around Jack Teas's shoulder; but then, just as I was watching them, he held Teas back by his belt, and I knew it was up to me.

I thought Dave Stone ought to have the touchdown because he'd played so hard after that kickoff fumble, so I called Forty-One—a give to the fullback going off the inside leg of the tackle.

Unfortunately, they had the blitz on; it just wasn't Dave's night.

Next I thought of little Mel Edmonds, whom I had disappointed on that first play and who was still in the game.

"Let's try yours again, Mel. Right, Formation One, Pass Three, X Circle. On first sound."

As I went back with the ball, I saw Mel take off like a shot, whirl, slip . . . and fall flat on his face in the wet grass. I looked for Skate, but he was covered in green, and just when I was wondering how this football was going to taste, I saw their big left end slip and fall, too, just as Mel had done. I swung out of the pocket to the right, shifted my 180 pounds of blubber into overdrive, and went over the goal line standing up.

Skate kicked the extra point for us, and we went back up the field to the sweet, sweet music of the stands.

"Stallings! Get 'em, Pete! Way to go, Stallings!"

The band was playing; Patsy and the other cheerleaders were leaping and cartwheeling like crazy along the track, and all at once it began to look easy again. We might beat these boys by a bunch of points. No real worries now; we had it going.

Excuse me again. Unbelievable as it may seem, we did not make another first down the whole third quarter.

I don't know what was wrong. Yes, I do know, too; I know three things. First, our timing was off something terrible. Stone and Foxx were either running into me on the hand-offs or coming by so wide and late that I felt like a man waiting for a streetcar. Second, we were playing a much better football team than anybody expected. If Greensboro had lost three games, it must have been the Vikings, the Colts, and the Miami Dolphins. Third, and most important of all, it continued to pour down rain, which made it hard for our receivers to run a crisp pattern, made it hard for me to see them, and made it hard for them to hold onto the ball when I did manage to get it to them. On one play I threw a perfect strike to our split end, Jake Grider, wide open and with a step on the cornerback, but it was as though I had thrown him a bar of soap. The ball was just too wet and slick to handle.

Our defensive line deserved a lot of credit though, especially Ike Mathis and our middle guard, Andy Holmes. If we couldn't move the ball, neither could Greensboro. It must have been a pretty dull contest from the fans' point of view. They were soaked by now, and cold, and all they had to look at was a bunch of stumblebums slogging back and forth at midfield.

26

I kept thinking to myself, "Any minute now he'll send in the option." It was getting late in the game, and so far about all we'd threatened them with was a bad cold and a sore throat. But each time the play came in, it was something else. A pass to Teas or Skate; Foxx to the weak side; Stone over right guard.

Finally, when we were about eight minutes into the last quarter, the rain slacked off a little and I connected on two passes, one to Grider and one to Foxx, that got us down to about their thirty-five. On the next play Foxx got twelve, but the gain was nullified by a holding penalty, and all at once we were back at midfield.

Edmonds came in with a play from the bench: the screen pass. We hadn't thrown it all night, and it caught them sound asleep. Big Dave bulled it all the way down to their twenty-two. I hate to say it, but Foxx probably would have gone all the way. Never mind, we were happy to be there. They really racked *me* up, though, after I had lobbed the ball to Stone; when we huddled again, I had a brassy taste in my mouth and my mouthpiece was gone. Maybe I swallowed it.

All of a sudden Teas punched his head into the huddle. "He wants you to try the draw, Pete."

"Quarterback Draw," I said. I didn't even hesitate. "First sound."

This time Billy Foxx's head wasn't the only one that came up in surprise. They all knew what play Dad wanted; and they all knew *I* knew. But they were a well-disciplined ball club, and they broke the huddle with the usual sharp clap of hands.

27

Bending over the center with my fingers fanned out under his big muddy rump, I suddenly knew I was going to break it all the way for the score. Don't ask me how I knew it—I just did. The rest is a sort of blur. I yelled "Hike!" and felt the ball slap into my hands, and at the same time I heard the pads popping along the line. I took my two steps back, pumped a fake to Grider, and in the next instant there it was—a big opening right down the middle of the field like the good Lord Himself had ordained it. Nothing between me and that goal-line stripe but some short, wet grass. In a way, though, it was like a nightmare—like those dreams where you're in slow motion and can't get going, or trying to run in waist-deep water at the swimming pool.

All I know is, I made it. Somehow I finally got down there. A guy came out of nowhere and launched into me from the side as I went in, but he was too late; I had six big ones for Morgan. A twenty-two-yard scamper by yours truly. It seemed like the whole team was down there to help me up, clapping me on the back, whooping and hollering like a tribe of Apaches.

The crowd? Well, they must have been cheering, too. The band must have been playing. But I'm not sure I heard any of it. There was new pressure now, real pressure. The score stood 14 to 13. We had to go for the two-point conversion if we meant to win this game.

I looked toward the bench to see if Edmonds was coming in with a play. No such luck. Dad was just standing there with his hands on his hips. And by the way, there was something about that I didn't like. He looked odd—sort of frozen. Was he sore? How could he be when I'd just made the TD?

28

In the huddle I spit cotton a couple of times, then gave them the play. "Right, Formation One, Thirty-three Lead.

"Billy," I said, "give it a real good shot. We've got to have two."

To my amazement Billy Foxx shook his head. "I can't do it, Pete. My shoulder's hurt. My whole right arm is numb."

"Run the roll-out, Pete," Dave Stone said in that big bass voice of his.

"Yeah, daddy," Skate chimed in. "You can do it, too!"

I looked up around the huddle at the other faces—wet, muddy, a couple of them slightly bloody—and what I saw told me it was all right. They were with me, so why not? After all, it was more for Dad than for me.

"OK, fellows, Big Nine to the right. Gimme all the help you can. This right here is the ball game."

Funny things happen. As it turned out, that really wasn't the ball game at all. Oh, I made the two points OK, crashing over the flag with a good two and a half inches to spare. The thing is, we still had three minutes of football left to play—which I apparently forgot all about.

I guess I got to listening too much to the crowd, or maybe the band. Something got in my eye. Maybe it was Patsy out there, whirling like a top with her blond hair swinging wet and heavy and her pleated skirt ballooning like a parachute. Or maybe I was looking at the scoreboard: Morgan 15, Greensboro 14, and thinking how all fifteen of those points belonged to me. What the heck, there was now less than a minute to play, and we had them stymied at their own thirty.

30

I expect you can guess what happened. Remember the play Dad diagrammed for us just before the start of the game? Remember where they start to the right and hand off to the end coming back around?

I saw it start. I even saw the quarterback hand the ball to the end—shoved it right in his gut. "End around," thinks Pete Stallings, the great fifteen-point-a-game quarterback. "If I can get up there fast, I can really bust him one." I felt like busting somebody now—show them how hardnosed I was. Win that cup.

But then I thought, wait a second, that's not an end around. He's going to throw the ball. Hold everything! What was that green blur that just went by me?

You guessed it. The flanker.

I made a quick turn, slipped . . . and did a Mel-Edmonds in the wet grass, flat on my face.

It was a beautiful pass, I have to admit. As Coach Dale warned us, the guy could really hum that seed. It went over my head at about twenty feet (I had a beautiful view, lying there in the grass), and there was the flanker running all alone, looking back over his shoulder and reaching up with both hands. When I think of it now, it seems to me he had a big smile on his face, but of course I couldn't really see his face that well.

They say when you're drowning, your whole life passes in front of your eyes in a flash. Something like that happened to me along about then—only it was the future that passed in front of my eyes, not the past. I seemed to see the scoreboard light up with six more points for Greensboro and us trooping back to the dressing room with our heads bowed in defeat—all because of my stupid mistake.

But then suddenly into my fishy gaze came another blur. Color this one orange. I saw a hand stretched out in desperation, just tipping the ball at the last possible instant— deflecting it enough that the flanker couldn't quite reach it.

Somebody had saved the game for us with a super effort, coming all the way across the field to bat the ball away. And that somebody was still sliding face-down in the wet grass like a guy on a bobsled. But I saw enough to read his number.

Billy Foxx.

3

Funny things happen. I know I said that once already, but you'll have to bear with me. It reminds me of all those jokes that start: "A funny thing happened on the way to . . ." Well, a funny thing happened to me on the way to the dressing room after the game—about four thousand loyal Morgan County fans forgot my name.

"Foxx!" they yelled. "Billy Foxx!"

Apparently all they remembered of a long, hard-fought, bruising football game was one play in the last forty seconds. A pretty short memory.

I know I must sound like a sorehead and maybe even a guy that would rather look good himself than see his team win a ball game. But that's not true. I was happy we won. I was grateful. And I'd be the last guy in the world to deny that Foxx made an absolutely fantastic save. It was one of the greatest defensive plays I ever saw, and it kept us from losing the game.

But it didn't *win* the game for us, did it? I mean, without those fifteen points we already had on the board, what difference would it have made?

Even in the dressing room it was the same. Oh, the guys came by and gave me a whack on the back and said, "Great game, Pete," but the big crowd was around Billy Foxx. Especially the crashers. The crashers are those certain fans that come down and manage to barge into the dressing room after a game. They're a special bunch—noncombatants, most of them, that never played a football game in their lives. They're the Section C quarterbacks that sit up there and scream for blood; really mean guys that like their football rough. The biggest thing they ever got hit by was a paper cup and a hotdog wrapper. Quinton Winters is one of them—one of the main ones. He was over there with his camera on a strap around his neck, asking Foxx a lot of questions and jotting down notes. Quinton's the sports editor of the local paper. He's up in his twenties now, but I remember when Quinton was in school; he played a mean clarinet in the marching band. Now he's an authority on the wishbone T and how hard a pulling guard ought to hit the end.

It surprised me a little, but after a while Billy Foxx disengaged himself from his idolators and came over to me.

"Pete," he said, "you were great tonight. Finest game you've played. Congratulations."

Maybe he meant it right, but it came out sounding wrong to me. It was as though the star were throwing the lowly peasant a bone. There was something patronizing about it, as if he were saying, "Keep up the good work, young fellow; you're finally showing some improvement." Me, who had played more football than he'd ever seen in his life counting TV with replays. I felt like telling him to bug off, but of course I didn't.

"You played fine, too, Billy. Great save." I nearly choked on that because it was me he saved—me and my stupidity. Sure, I was partly to blame for my troubles. I don't deny it.

"How's the shoulder?" I said.

"Huh?"

"Your shoulder. You said you hurt it."

"Oh, that—it's OK, nothing serious."

I got busy unlacing my pads, and he left.

After a game Dad usually has a few choice remarks to make about our performance. If we lost, he'd tell us not to get downhearted and then point out our mistakes. If we won, he'd congratulate us and then point out our mistakes. But tonight for some reason he got busy with the equipment and let us go without the usual postmortem.

I was glad to get out of there myself. It was too hot, too steamy, and the crashers had filled the place up with cigar smoke. I even got annoyed with Skate and his jive talk.

"Going down to the Cave, Pete?"

I had hesitated there under the eave of the building, watching the rain falling in the parking lot, and when I turned around, I was surprised to see Billy Foxx standing beside me. He had some books under his arm and was wearing that old army-surplus fatigue jacket he wears a lot.

"I don't know," I said. "I've got a date. Whatever she wants to do, I guess."

I knew what he wanted. He wanted me to give him a ride home.

He shrugged. "I thought maybe if you were headed down Kyle . . ."

35

"Maybe Quinton Winters will give you a lift," I said, and dodged off through the rain to my jeep.

Actually, I felt a little bad about that later. I had cut the guy in a personal way, which it wasn't like me to do; but he was in my hair so bad that I couldn't help myself.

When I got to Patsy's house, she wasn't ready, so I had to sit in the living room and talk to her folks while she changed into dry clothes and did something to her hair. This irked me a little, too. It's not that I mind her folks— they're nice enough in a icky, old-fashioned sort of way— but they're very strict with her and won't let her stay out past twelve o'clock. It was already close to eleven, which meant we'd have only about an hour before I had to bring her back. Pat knew this, too, and yet she was in there with the record player going, dawdling around and messing with her hair as if she had all night. I even got the idea she was deliberately stalling, just so we *wouldn't* have long together.

Mrs. Lloyd wanted to fix me a cup of hot chocolate (which is something I gave up back about the time I gave up bubble gum and shooting marbles), and Mr. Lloyd wanted to talk to me about football. Mr. Lloyd must think football is the only subject I'm mentally competent to discuss because he never talks to me about anything else. He usually starts with a few remarks about the latest game; but that's only for openers. What he really likes to talk about is back when *he* played ball, and it doesn't take him long to swing the conversation around to the good old single wing. According to Mr. Lloyd's view, the game has deteriorated quite a bit in the past thirty years.

"Football was a rugged game in my day, Pete," he says,

implying, I suppose, that what we play today is more on the order of a pillow fight in the girls' dorm. "Why, we didn't even wear face guards."

He expects this to amaze me—though why, I can't imagine, since he's told me so himself half a dozen times before.

"There was hardly a guy in the line that didn't have a few teeth missing. And plastic helmets? We never heard of them. The old leather jobs, that's all we had to wear. I remember one time . . . ."

During all this the Lloyds' cocker spaniel came in and began to untie my shoelaces by grabbing them in his teeth, backing hard, and throwing his head from side to side. I didn't mind that too much, but by the time Mr. Lloyd got around to his story about drop-kicking a field goal, the dog had finished with the shoestrings and was starting in on the cuffs of my new double-knit trousers.

Finally, after I had declined two more cups of hot chocolate and heard a replay of the entire 1944 season, Patsy came out looking like an early warning system—her hair full of those big spring-shaped curlers. It just wasn't my night.

"I can't go anywhere looking like this," she said, "but we could drive down to the Cave and drink a shake in the car."

"Isn't it raining?" Mrs. Lloyd asked. I guess she figured that would be an extremely dangerous thing to do in the rain.

"Just be sure to get home by twelve," said Mr. Lloyd, and all at once the rash and reckless old drop-kicker was back in his role of father.

I retied my wet shoelaces, dried my hands on the sofa, and we left.

Outside in the jeep, Patsy leaned over and gave me a kiss on the cheek, but then held me off when I tried to put my arms around her. "Remember the hair," she said. "I spent too long fixing it."

"You sure did."

"Don't be grumpy. Lordy, didn't it rain, though? I was wet clear through to my unmentionables."

I've noticed she has a way of teasing you a little with words like "unmentionables."

"Yeah," I said. "I got a little damp myself."

"By the way, Pete, you were wonderful tonight. I was so proud of you, I got tears in my eyes."

"Thanks, Pat."

She put her hand over mine and gave it a squeeze.

We drove down to the Cave, me feeling a little better.

As you may have guessed, the Cave is where the kids my age hang out. It's a shake place, and you can get hamburgers, hotdogs, pizzas, etc. There's a jukebox inside with speakers wired outside under the eaves so the music blares out over the parking lot, and when the weather isn't too cold or wet, there'll be as many kids outside milling around the cars as there are inside. In the summer they even dance out there sometimes, though it's supposed to be against the law. On most nights—and particularly after a game—the Cave is a pretty lively place. If there was somebody you were trying to find, the Cave is the first place you'd go to look for them.

When Patsy and I steamed up in my old jeep, we saw Jack Teas and Angy Edmonds sitting in Jack's fancy blue Camaro like an orchid in a cabbage patch. By that I mean Jack's car stood out slightly among all the beat-up second-hand jalopies the other guys were driving. Jack happens to be from the richest family in town—they own the hosiery mill—and the only reason he doesn't drive a Cadillac is because he *prefers* a smaller, sportier car. He also has a dune buggy for summer fun. Anything Jack wants, Jack gets. And generally speaking, what Jack wants is the best of everything. Even his golf clubs are Haig Ultras. Now, you may be thinking that with all his dough and all this indulgence on the part of his parents, Jack could be a pretty sizable pain in the neck. He could be; but he isn't. I don't think there's a more popular boy in school than Jack Teas. It would be easy to resent him if he were any kind of guy except the kind he is. This may surprise you, but to me Jack is an awful lot like Skate Baker. I've often thought to myself that the only differences between John Robert Teas III and Skate Baker I are the color of their skins and about half a million bucks. (It may be two million bucks, but half a million is as high as my mind goes.) In just about every other way they're soul brothers. And by saying that I don't mean to put either of them down. They're both great guys, good athletes, and . . . well, swingers. Of course while Jack's playing golf at the country club, Skate is sacking groceries at the A & P, but neither of them had anything to do with that. That's life. They like each other and they understand each other. In the locker room they even have a way of talking together that the rest of us don't always understand. For example, one afternoon Skate showed up for practice wearing a new pair of shoes, very fancy ones.

"Hey, man, fine kicks," Teas said to him. "What are they?"

"Discount store specials."

"You gotta be kidding. Ray Charles couldn't afford shoes like that. Take me to your leader."

"Eldridge Cleaver?"

They both laughed, and I'm still not sure what was funny.

Anyway, when Patsy and I crashed at the Cave in my old heap, there sat Jack and Angy Edmonds (who is Mel's twin sister), and they motioned us to come over and join them. This suited us fine since the jeep leaks and the heater doesn't work half the time. Pat wanted a malted and an order of fries, which I went in to get, and when I came back to the car, the two girls were gassing about the awards dinner and the big dance that always follows the last game of the season. This was about the worst subject they could have picked as far as I was concerned. Any minute I expected somebody to say, "Who you suppose will get Most Valuable Player?"

But mainly they were talking about the dance and the dresses they were planning to wear. Angy was debating hot pants, if they were allowed; Patsy said her mother was making her a long dress with a split up the side of the leg. Something called a cheongsam. If I knew her mother as I thought I did, that split wasn't coming very far up the side of anybody's leg. It also occurred to me that Pat was taking a good bit for granted since I hadn't even asked her yet to be my date. But of course I would ask her. She had a right to expect that because neither of us had dated anyone else for nearly a year.

Finally there was a gap in the female chatter, and Jack got a few words in edgewise. "You heard about Baxter's monster man?"

"I heard they had a good one," I said, "and he's only a junior."

"According to Quinton Winters, he's had locks on all-state since the middle of the season. By the way, they walloped Fairbanks tonight, thirty-three to zip."

I whistled. "That makes them about a twenty-point favorite over us."

"Mathematically speaking."

"We can still take them."

"Sure. But not like we played tonight."

"What's a monster man?" Angy asked. They watch these games, and half the time I don't think they know what's going on.

"A monster man," said Jack, "is a roving linebacker. He calls the defense and positions himself anywhere along the line he wants to—in other words, wherever he thinks the play is coming. This guy we're talking about weighs two hundred and twenty pounds, and they say he's a real headhunter."

"So what's a headhunter?"

"A guy that likes to stick you. A hard tackler."

I knew why Jack dreaded Baxter's monster man. Playing at flanker, he'd be trying to block this guy during a big part of the game—especially on the triple option. But if anybody could do it, Jack Teas could.

We talked on for a while, about first one thing and another, and before long it was time to take Patsy home. We parked in front of her house, and this time she forgot about the hair curlers for a minute—but only for a minute, because a light came on at the bedroom window and the old drop-kicker peered out between the curtains.

"You know something?" I said. "Your old man must have been a real heller in his day."

"What makes you say that?"

"Why else would he be so suspicious?"

She suddenly sneezed, then laughed, and gave me another kiss that was flavored with chocolate malt and French fries. I didn't mind. She was quite a gal.

"You still with me, Pat?"

"Of course I am. What a dopey thing to say! You know how I feel about you, Pete."

"Good night, doll."

"Night, Pete."

Then she was gone, running toward the door through the rain with her raincoat held over her head like Bela Lugosi doing the vampire act.

When I got home, I was surprised to see the light still on in Dad's study. He usually went to bed early on the night of a game; it sapped him a little, I guess. But tonight there he was, still up, still drinking coffee.

I got myself a glass of milk and a hunk of cake in the kitchen, then wandered in to see what he was doing.

"Hi, Pete. You're home early, aren't you?"

"It's after twelve."

"Is it?" He looked surprised. He also looked worried and

tired. "Did you hear the score of the Baxter-Fairbanks game?"

"Yeah, Baxter really creamed them, didn't they? I guess we'll be going in as the underdog."

"We would have anyhow. Baxter has a seventeen-game streak working. Nearly two seasons now since they lost a ball game."

"Teas is worried about their monster man."

"McClendon?"

"I didn't know his name."

"You'll know it next Friday night. All in all, he's probably the best football player we'll face this season. His specialty, by the way, is breaking up the option. He's a one-man gang out there."

"He hasn't seen our option yet."

"Maybe he has and maybe he hasn't."

"How do you mean?"

"We've got films of them; maybe they've got films of us, too."

"Well," I said, "ours is a *triple* option. He probably hasn't seen much of that. If he stops Foxx, I'll give it to Stone; if he stops Stone, I'll keep it myself."

"You mean like you did tonight?"

Something about the way he said that caused the cake to turn dry in my mouth, and a tingling sensation went over my scalp. So this was why he had stayed up, waiting for me.

"Hey, just a sec, Dad. We weren't supposed to run the option, remember?"

"I wasn't referring to that."

"Well, what are you referring to? I ran Foxx plenty tonight. And when we went for the two-point conversion, I offered him the ball and he wouldn't take it. Said his shoulder was hurt. You can ask anybody in the huddle."

"I don't question that, Pete. But when I sent in the draw play, why did you keep the ball yourself? We haven't run a quarterback draw three times this season."

"Well, maybe we should have run it more," I said. "It put six points on the board, didn't it?"

"For your information," he said in a cold, tight voice, "the reason the play worked was because Skate clipped the halfback. The referees either didn't see it or just didn't call it. Instead of six points, we should have had a fifteen-yard penalty."

I stood there staring at him. My scalp was really prickling now, and my face felt red hot.

"Furthermore," he went on, "you almost cost us the game by getting sucked in on a play that I practically preached a sermon about, five minutes before we went on the field."

"I slipped and fell."

"You were sucked in!" he said sharply.

I was standing there with a glass of milk in one hand and half a piece of cake in the other. The rest of the cake was stuck in my throat somewhere.

When I finally managed to speak, I couldn't keep the hurt, bitter sarcasm out of my voice. "Aside from that," I said, "how did I grade?"

"Aside from that," he said, "you played a mediocre game of football. From now on you'll play the left cornerback on defense. I want Billy Foxx at safety."

44

4

Once when I was a little kid just five years old, I wanted to do something nice for my dad. It was his birthday—or maybe Father's Day, I don't remember which —and I racked my brain to think of something that would really please him. I could have bought him a present, of course, but I wanted this to be something special from me to him, not just a necktie or a shirt that Mom would probably pick out and then pay for with money that was his own money anyway. Besides, the only thing he really wanted was a new set of golf clubs, which was too much to spend. Mom said I ought to paint him a picture, and she'd frame it for me. At kindergarten we were hitting the artwork pretty hard—you know, drawing houses with black smoke curling out of the chimney, and trees that looked like a cannon ball on top of an over-ripe banana. I gave it some thought, but then I hit on what I considered to be an even better idea. If Dad wanted a new set of golf clubs, and I was so handy with the pigments, why not just dress up his old ones for him? I even knew where there was half a can of pink enamel that Mom had used to paint the bathroom shutters.

Unfortunately, I neglected to discuss the plan with my mother before putting it into effect. I wanted it to be a complete surprise—which it was.

"What in the name of heaven has this little idiot done?"

That was his initial reaction. His secondary reaction was even more colorful because I had put the clubs back in the bag before they were dry, and all the heads were stuck together. He couldn't even pull them apart.

The story sounds funny now from a distance of thirteen years. I've even heard Dad tell it and laugh. But he didn't laugh that day, and neither did I. I went up to my room and cried my eyes out because he had hurt my feelings— really mangled them—over something that was meant to be a gesture of love.

Now, I'd be overstating it by quite a bit if I told you I felt the same way that night after our little row in the study —after all, I'm an eighteen-year-old idiot now, not five. But at the same time there are certain parallels about it. The man just couldn't seem to understand that everything I did out there on that football field was for him, not me. I didn't care a hang about that gold cup personally. In fact, I was beginning to wish I'd never heard of the damn thing.

Still, I had to walk right past it there on the mantel to get up to my room that night.

It was a long time before I finally went to sleep, but when I did, I must have slept like a dead man. It was nearly noon when I woke up the next morning. The phone woke me, and at first I thought it might be Patsy, but it wasn't. It was the vicar calling Mom to remind her that to-morrow was her day to fix the altar. That much I could make out from just hearing her end of the conversation.

I rolled out of bed and took inventory of the old phy-sique. There was the usual stiffness and soreness, and also a couple of things I hadn't noticed the night before. The in-side of my lower lip was cut, and there was a big raw strawberry on my left elbow that my pajama sleeve had stuck to during the night. I had to soak it in warm water to get it loose. There was also a mild feeling of depression left over from the scene with Dad. As soon as Mom was off the horn, I phoned Patsy for a little cheering up.

"Hello, Pete."

"What are we doing tonight?" I said. "There's a good show at the Ritz."

"Gee, I guess I won't be able to go out."

"What for?"

"Can't you tell? I've come down with a terrible cold in my nose." She was so stuffed up that it came out sounding like "coded by doze."

"Great," I said, "that blows the whole weekend!"

"Well!" she said huffily. "Please forgive me for causing you such inconvenience."

"I'm sorry, Pat. I didn't mean that the way it sounded. You know I'm sorry you're sick—it's just too bad we can't go out. Can I bring you something? A book to read? Some ice cream from the drugstore?"

It took a while to smooth her out, but I finally did. She didn't want me to come over, though. I might catch her cold, she said, and not be able to play in the big game next

week. Like heck. It would take more than a runny nose to keep me out of *that* game. But of course I didn't say that to her; she was only trying to be thoughtful.

We chatted for a little while, but she was sniffling and sneezing all the time and I finally told her to go back to bed. What I had in mind was to send her one of those kooky get-well cards they had at Sloan's.

Mom evidently heard me stirring because by the time I got dressed and went downstairs, she had me a plate of ham and eggs ready, with pancakes on the side. I wasn't really all that hungry, but I pretended to be pleased so as not to disappoint her. I spend a lot of my time trying not to disappoint folks.

"I thought you played an outstanding game last night, Pete," she said. "I was awful proud of you."

"Dad wasn't."

"Oh?"

"Mediocre. I believe that's the word he used."

"Well, of all things!" She looked really distressed at that. "You most certainly were not mediocre, Pete, and you never have been. I can't imagine why he'd say a thing like that. It's not like your father. Not like him at all."

"Where's the paper, Mom?"

She handed me the *Times*.

"No, I meant the *Morgan County Gazette*."

She knew what I wanted. I wanted to read what Quinton Winters said about the game.

"Let me see," she said, "what did I do with that *Gazette*? Oh, now I remember. Pete, I'm sorry, but I think I wrapped the garbage in it."

49

A brand-new paper that hadn't been in the house three hours.

I shouldn't have done it, but I was in no mood to be mothered and protected. I got up from the table, opened the cabinet under the sink, and pulled out the garbage pail.

"Pete."

Sure enough, right there in a three-column picture covered with coffee grounds and bacon grease was my good friend Billy Foxx just tipping that ball away. Exhibit A. And right there on his belly in the grass—like a seal waiting for somebody to throw him a fish—was yours truly. Exhibit B. The headline on the story went: FOXX SHINES AGAIN.

I didn't say anything, just shoved it all back in the can and sat down to try and finish my breakfast. But it was no use. It was like trying to swallow that cake last night.

"Mom," I said.

"Yes, Pete?"

"I'd like to do something nice for Dad. Is there any of that pink enamel left?"

It was a stroke of pure genius. It broke us up. We both laughed till we cried.

By the way, in case I forgot to mention it . . . I think a lot of my mom.

Dad had gone hunting, she told me, with Coach Dale and Dave Stone's father. It had turned out to be a beautiful day, but still too wet from last night's rain to rake the yard, so I washed some windows for Mom till around two o'clock, and then she gave me a grocery list to take down to the A & P.

I had most of the stuff in the buggy and was headed toward the check-out counter when somebody punched my shoulder. I looked around and there was Skate, wearing his white apron and a little black plastic bow tie.

"Cut it out, Skate. I got enough bruises already."

He was grinning down at me from six feet three—the three being mostly hair. "Pete," he said, "I got some fantabulous news. I swear you won't believe it. Guess who phoned me after the game last night?"

"No idea, Skate, who?"

"The head coach at N.C. State."

"You're kidding!"

"Scout honor. The phone was ringing when I opened the door."

I was amazed. "What did he say?"

Skate let his face collapse then exactly the way Godfrey Cambridge does, or Flip Wilson. "Three hoggies and a swiss-on-rye. He thought he dialed the Eighth Avenue Delicatessen."

I grabbed the buggy and tried to shove it on, but he held me back, laughing.

"Hey, man, don't split yet. I want to talk to you about something serious. No jive, now. Something serious."

"Yeah, I bet."

"Pete, when I say no jive, I mean it, don't I? Look in these baby blues of mine and tell me what you see."

I looked in his eyes—which are actually chocolate brown of course and not blue at all—and sure enough, Skate Baker was serious. It's the only way you can ever be certain.

"All right, so what's on your mind?"

"You know we're buddies, Pete." Ominous.

"Skate, for crying out loud . . . "

"OK, here it comes." He fidgeted with that little tie for a minute and looked around the store like a shoplifter about to make a lift—in other words, nervous. That really did get to me because I never saw him that way before, not even before a game.

"I'm all ears, Skate. Tuned to Serious."

"Don't cut me, man. I got this to say because they sort of elected me. I don't like it either. But they figured if any-body could say it to you, I could. Right?"

"Who's 'they'?"

"The team. Most of the guys."

"Oh. A soul session."

"Don't cut me, Pete."

"I'm sorry, Skate."

He hesitated again; licked those thick lips of his. "Billy Foxx," he said. "Name's familiar, right?"

"Yeah, there was something about him in the *Gazette* this morning—I forget what."

"Pete, Billy Foxx ain't half as bad a guy as you seem to think he is."

"Is that the consensus?"

"I don't know about the consensus, but that's how most of us feel."

"Go on."

"Well, you don't seem to dig him anymore. It's like he turns you off. Like he's Lawrence Welk and you're O. C. Smith."

I had to laugh at that. But at least he made me O. C. Smith.

"Well, I'm making bananas of this, but what I'm trying to say is we like you both, Pete. We think you're both great guys, great ball players, and we want you working *together*, man. For the sake of the team. For the sake of every-damn-body."

"Baker!" It was the store manager.

"Yes, sir!"

"We can use you up front, if you can spare the time."

"He's getting my bottle returns," I said, and gave the creep a look that sent him back to the checkout.

"Skate . . ."

"I'm listening, Pete."

I opened my mouth again, but nothing came out. What could I say? How could I make them understand? It wasn't really Billy Foxx; it was that gold cup. My dad. I was in a crazy, complicated situation none of them could possibly understand. It went too far back—had too many angles.

"Skate," I said again.

"Still listening, man. *All* ears."

"It'll be OK. Believe me. Can we leave it at that?"

"Pete, I'm with you, babe. I'd break the guy's arm if you told me to. I ain't saying I'd be *happy* to do it, but me and you been pals too long."

I looked at him—into those baby blues that were really chocolate brown—and said: "Skate, I got problems that are hard to talk about, know what I mean? It has to do with my dad. But I promise you this. We'll beat Baxter, and we'll . . ."

He shook his head impatiently. "Hell with Baxter. Sure, we'll beat Baxter, but hell with Baxter, Pete."

"OK, OK, OK. Skate, will you listen?"

53

"It's your nickel."

"Just trust me."

"Didn't I ever?"

"Now you're cutting me, you jungle bunny."

He took a deep breath, and it came back a sigh. "Sure, I trust you, Pete. Who else?"

I started off with my buggy again, then stopped and turned back to him.

"By the way," I said. "Dad told me about that clip last night. He said I wouldn't have made the TD except you clipped the halfback."

"White man speak with forked tongue," said Skate. "Me no clip halfback. Clip linebacker."

5

Being without a date on Saturday night is like suiting up for a football game and then having to sit the whole thing out on the bench. You're all primed and ready, but all you can do is watch. At first I thought I would just stay home and either work on my science project or write that theme that was due in English, but Mom and Dad had gone out somewhere to play bridge, and the house was too quiet. I can't concentrate when it's too quiet. If there's anything that destroys my concentration, it's absolute quiet. I put a stack of Beatle records on the stereo, turned the volume up good and high, and got out my notes on Walden Pond. But somehow that didn't do it either. Finally I gave up and went down to the Cave.

The first people I saw were Ike Mathis and Kitty Bell, sitting in Ike's old Model A with the flowers and peace symbols painted all over it. In case I didn't mention it before, Ike plays center on the team, and he's the biggest guy on the squad. He's the biggest guy in school, for that matter. Ike checks in at 235, and he's not much taller than me, which means he's built roughly on the order of a bale of cotton. When he crawls into that old Ford of his, the thing lists way over to the side like a boat about to capsize. In fact, the car has a permanent tilt to it from all that weight on the driver's side. Ike and Kitty make a funny-looking couple because Kitty's no bigger than a bird—she even acts like a bird, fluttering and twittering constantly. They say opposites attract, and I guess that's the case with Ike and Kitty.

Naturally, the first thing they wanted to know is where is Patsy. I told them she was home, sick with a cold.

"Angy must have a cold, too," Kitty said. "Here comes Jack Teas without a date."

We looked around and saw Jack's blue Camaro swing up to the curb.

"Wrong," Ike said. "He's dating Dave Stone tonight."

Big Dave was in the front seat with Jack where Angy would normally be. They got out and came over to us.

"Hey, you guys," said Teas, "want to go to Elkton with us?"

"What for?"

"The Rubber Souls are playing at the 500 Club tonight. Me and Dave thought we'd drive over and give a listen."

"Where's Angy?" Kitty asked.

"Grounded," Jack said gloomily. "I got her home too late last night, and she can't go out the rest of the week."

"Tough."

"Well, I blew it. It was my own fault. But what do you say—going with us?"

"They won't let us in at the 500 Club," Kitty said. "The place serves liquor, and you have to be twenty-one."

56

The 500 was a supper club over near Elkton, eighteen miles from Morgan. On weekends they had live music, and the Rubber Souls were a group we all liked. I had a couple of their records.

"We look pretty close to twenty-one," Jack said. "Especially Ike and Dave. Besides, I've been there before. I know they'll let us in."

Ike was already shaking his head. "I can't swing it, Jack. There's a big cover charge, and then they expect you to order something to eat. It could run eight or ten bucks."

"I'll pay the cover myself," Jack said.

But Ike was still shaking his head. I think Kitty sort of wanted to go, but when she saw that Ike was against it, she was against it, too. "I'd rather go to the show," she said. "It's Paul Newman."

"Yeah, but the Rubber Souls are live, man. Come on, what do you say? Have you home by twelve-thirty or one."

"Nope. Thanks but no thanks."

"Pete?" He turned to me.

"I don't think so, Jack."

"Aw, come on, man. What else is there to do? You're stag, aren't you?"

"Did you ever notice," Kitty went on, "how much Paul Newman looks like Billy Foxx? His eyes and all?"

I guess that's what did it, her bringing up Foxx's name at just that moment. Anyway, something caused me to change my mind, even though I didn't really want to—even though it was against my better judgment.

"Sure, count me in," I said. "But I'll have to go home and get a tie."

Teas slapped me on the back. "No, you won't either," he said. "I've got an extra one in the car."

The 500 Club was really more of a roadhouse than what you'd normally think of as a supper club, even though they did serve food. It was somewhere between a honky-tonk and a nightclub—a big frame building just off the side of the highway with neon running all the way around the edge of the roof and colored lights strung up in the parking lot. There were two entrances: one to the bar and one to the main room, where the tables were crowded around the dance floor with checkered tablecloths on them and candles in hurricane lamps. When we got there, the band was playing, and even from the parking lot you didn't miss a note. Acid rock. It was like the walls of the building bulged a little with every beat.

Inside, it wasn't only deafening—it stunned you a little. Communication was mainly by sign language. We paid the three-dollar cover charge at the door, and a woman wearing a blond wig and a red jump suit stamped "500" on the backs of our hands with a rubber stamp the way they postmark a letter at the post office. I guess that was so if anybody had to go outside for a minute to get some fresh air or clear their ears, they could prove they'd already paid the cover when they came back in. The place was full of people and smoke and motion, but it was so dark that it all sort of ran together—nightmarish, in a way. Unreal, as Skate would say. But it was exciting. The Rubber Souls were up there, squirming and shouting and banging those electric guitars, and out on the floor the couples were squared off and circling around each other like a bunch of karate experts

58

looking for an opening to attack. What surprised me more than anything was the crowd. I guess I was expecting to see teen-agers and young couples, but most of these people were oldies—thirty-five, forty, some of them even older than that. It bugged me a little to see people out there the age of Mom and Dad, horsing around like a bunch of kids. One old bald-headed guy was really having fun. "He's not cutting a rug," Jack said, "he's cutting a wall-to-wall carpet. The coronary two-step!"

They gave us a table near the back wall, and Dave and I ordered a Coke. Jack called for a bottle of beer. When he saw me looking at him, he gave a shrug and leaned over the hurricane lamp to shout something at me, but I couldn't hear what he said. The music was too loud. Well, I wasn't going to grouse about it. One beer isn't going to make anybody drunk, and for all I knew, they might ask us to leave if we only sat there drinking Cokes. The music was great, and I was enjoying it.

It must have been around ten o'clock when the band finished the first set and went out for a break, and that was really the first time it had been quiet enough to talk.

"Gee, I wish Ike and Kitty had come along," Teas said.

"Aren't you enjoying it?"

"Yeah, but we need a bird or two. With Kitty along, we'd have had somebody to dance with. There's not a soul in the place I know."

"Well, I hate to contradict you," Dave Stone said, "but there's a party of folks from Morgan over there at the corner table. And if I'm not mistaken, one of them is about to pay us a visit."

"Somebody we know?"

"You know Quinton Winters, don't you?"

"Oh, mother."

We looked around, and sure enough, a guy in one of those Edwardian suits was bearing down on us, making his way unsteadily between the tables with a silly grin on his face. It was none other than Quinton, the old sports editor, and he looked as if he was feeling no pain. In fact, he was bringing his whisky glass with him.

"Well, well, well, well. If it's not the four horsemen of the Apocalypse! Oops, no, I see I am mistaken. One of your number is missing. We have here only three-fourths of the Morgan County backfield. Where's the vulpine one? Or don't you guys associate with neophytes?"

"Hello, Quinton," Jack said. "Have a seat and join us. Take a load off your feet."

I don't think Quinton even caught the sarcasm in the way Jack said it. By "load" he meant "package."

Quinton sat down and leaned both elbows on the table. "Tell me, boys," he said, "are you celebrating the Greensboro debacle or getting in shape for Baxter?"

"Neither," said Dave. "We came over to hear the music."

"But of course. After all, there wasn't much to celebrate about the Greensboro game, was there? And as for Baxter . . ." He frowned and shook his head, then looked up and smiled. "But I don't want to spoil your evening by bringing that up."

"Don't you think we can beat Baxter?" I asked.

He turned his head and looked at me as if he had just noticed I was sitting there. "If you read my column this morning, you already know what I think of your chances against Baxter."

"I haven't seen the paper yet," I said. It was on the tip of my tongue to tell him Mom wrapped the garbage in it, but there's no point in doing something like that.

"Well, when you get around to it," he said sarcastically, "it may interest you to see what I had to say about your own performance last night. Actually, I didn't think you did too badly."

"Thanks a lot. That's very generous of you, Quint, since it was me that put all fifteen points on the board."

When I said that, out of the corner of my eye I saw Dave and Jack exchange a glance. Quinton had a surprised expression, too—a look of pleased surprise, like when a fisherman sees his cork go under.

"That's odd," he said. "I'm aware that you made two touchdowns and a two-point conversion, but that only adds up to fourteen. I was under the impression that Skate Baker kicked an extra point."

All at once I felt my face turn red and my ears start to pound. He was right of course. What a stupe! I'd forgotten all about Skate's kick, and for twenty-four hours I'd been going around taking all the credit for having won the game single-handed. I was really hacked—especially because Jack and Dave were there and heard me say it.

Quinton got out a cigarette and lit it, giving us all plenty of time to enjoy my embarrassment. Finally he said: "And by the way, Stallings, what happened to the triple option? Did you tear that page out of your play book?"

"No, it's still in there."

"You didn't use it any against Greensboro."

"Dad told me not to."

"I wonder why." He took a sip of his drink. "It would have been nice to see Foxx carry the ball once in a while —especially when we were fourteen points behind."

I was burning now. "Foxx carried the ball all he wanted to," I said. "He even turned it down on one particular play when we really needed him."

Quinton gave that little smirk of his, gazing down into his drink. "I guess he was afraid he'd get benched—can't afford to outshine the coach's son."

"Hey, cut it out, Winters," Dave said. "That was a low blow and you know it."

"Yeah," said Jack. "Can that kind of crap."

Quinton shrugged it off, cool as a cucumber. "I'm only repeating what I've heard said around town."

"By who?" I said. "Some football expert like yourself that never played a game in his life?" I was about ready to swing on the guy.

He took another slow, deliberate sip of his drink.

"It's true I never played football," he said. "I don't play golf either. But I can still tell when Arnold Palmer hits a bad shot."

That sounded to me like an answer he'd had ready for a long time.

"Can I buy you fellows another round of beer?"

"You can do us an even bigger favor," Jack said. "Evaporate."

He got up, still smirking that smirk of his. "No hard feelings, guys. Just thought I'd cast these pearls before you.

And don't worry too much about Baxter. Foxx will probably pull it out."

As soon as he was gone, Jack poured the rest of his beer in a glass and said: "Let's just pretend that never happened."

"Yeah," said Dave. "It's all over now and forgotten."

Brother, was he ever wrong.

6

The next morning at church I had a revelation. Not exactly a religious revelation, but one of those moments when everything comes clear and you get a fresh perspective on all your problems and hang-ups.

There was a bird singing outside the church window, and all of a sudden I found myself remembering a parrakeet that Patsy once had. They kept it in a cage at night, but during the day this bird was allowed to fly around anywhere in the house it wanted to, though never outside because that would be too dangerous. (The cat finally caught it and ate it anyway, but that's not the point of my telling this.) Peetie was what the Lloyds called him, and Peetie was very tame. You could carry him around on your finger or your shoulder, and he seemed to be a very happy, well-adjusted bird, although there's no way to look in a bird's face and tell his mood. He had a good home and plenty to eat, and he was well treated (except of course by the cat). But Peetie had one habit that made me wonder if he was really happy. He used to spend an awful lot of time perched on the frame of the dining-room mirror, looking at himself. He'd chirp at himself, try to peck himself, and sometimes even back off and fly against the glass as if he were trying to break through to the other side.

"The bird has a Narcissus complex," Mr. Lloyd used to say, which he explained to me as meaning the bird was infatuated with his own image.

I had another idea about it myself. I had an idea that poor little guy might be lonely. I thought it was just possible that he had a desperate longing to be with other birds of his own kind. Here he was, living in a world of people, and everybody assumed that because we liked it, he liked it, too.

By now you must be wondering how on earth this story of the bird relates to me and my revelation. All right, two ways: First, I seemed to see a parallel between myself and that bird in that we were both being tricked by an illusion. What the bird saw in the mirror wasn't really another bird —it was an image he created himself by perching in front of it. Do you get what I mean? To turn the thing around, maybe when I looked at Billy Foxx, I wasn't seeing the guy himself as he really was; maybe I was seeing a false image I had created my own self in my own mind.

Second, I saw a parallel between Billy Foxx and the bird. I had been assuming that just because Foxx had become a big star on the football team and the crowds cheered for him, he was happy and well contented with the whole situation. Yet our personal friendship had fallen apart because of it. And I knew darn well that at one time

Billy Foxx liked me better than any other boy in town. To carry it a little further—and I may be getting ridiculous now, but this is what I was thinking in church—I thought maybe when Foxx came up to me and said, "Fine game, Pete," or hinted he wanted a ride in my jeep, he was flying against a glass and couldn't break through.

"Take a look at yourself," I said to myself. "Who has really changed, you or Foxx?" Only last night I was bragging about winning the game against Greensboro when Skate Baker might just as well have argued that it was *his* point that made the difference. Except of course Skate would never think to suggest a thing like that. With all his jiving and kidding around, a boast like that would never even have occurred to him.

Me, Pete Stallings, I'm the guy it occurred to.

So right there, kneeling in the Episcopal Church, I made a resolve to get myself in line and stop acting like a spoiled brat. I was going to take a fresh look at Billy Foxx and our whole relationship.

As it turned out, I had a chance to take a fresh look at him about thirty minutes later. As we were driving home, we passed the Methodist Church, and there in the crowd at the foot of the steps I saw Foxx chatting with a girl whose hairdo looked familiar.

"Well, I see Patsy's cold is better," Mom said. "She was able to go to church."

"Yeah, apparently so."

The old resolve took a little bit of a beating right there, but in the end it held firm. After all, Pat and Billy did go to the same church, and it was only natural they might meet

66

and chat together when the service was over. This was the New Me thinking. Besides, one swallow doesn't make a summer—nor one parrakeet a winter.

I waited till after lunch, and then I gave Patsy a buzz.

"Hello, deah," I said, using my Amos and Andy voice. "How's the cold?"

"It's better," she said. "But I'm still not over it yet."

"I saw you at church."

"Yeah." She didn't elaborate—just yawned into the phone like an audio of Hurricane Camille coming into the Gulf.

"I wake you up or something?"

"No. No, I was awake, just sitting here reading the Sundays."

"What's my horoscope?" She was big on horoscopes, and I knew she would have read it by now—mine and everybody else's whose birthday she knew.

"Hold it a second," she said, and I heard her rattling the papers. "Here we are—Scorpio. Says, 'Recognize end of situation or relationship. Now is time to finish rather than initiate projects. Message will become increasingly clear. Visit one confined to home or hospital.' "

"By the way, did you get my card?"

"What card?"

"One of those nutty get-well cards from Sloan's. I mailed it yesterday."

"How could I get it on Sunday?"

"That's right, I forgot. I think I also forgot to put on a stamp. It'll probably arrive postage due."

"Well, at least you didn't send flowers. I couldn't afford a dozen roses, collect."

"Hey, are you sore or something?"

"No, you chump, just kidding. It was sweet of you to think of the card, even though it's going to cost me eight cents when it gets here."

"Well, how about if I drop by this afternoon? I'll bring your eight cents back."

"You really think you ought to, Pete?"

"Why not?"

"Well, I've still got a pretty bad cold. What if you caught it from me?"

I started to tell her I was no more susceptible to colds than Billy Foxx, but then I remembered the New Me and the Big Resolve. "Don't worry about that. Besides, we can't smooch with the old drop-kicker lurking back there behind the potted plants."

She laughed at that, which encouraged me a little. "Tell you what," she said. "Why don't you wait and come around five? Dad said something about driving out to Grandmother's this afternoon for a while."

"Five it is, then."

"See you, Pete."

"Bye, doll."

Dad had asked us to come to the gym at two o'clock on Sunday afternoon and have a look at the Baxter film. It wasn't compulsory—he planned to show it again on Monday and Tuesday—but most of the guys turned up. Like me, I guess they were anxious to see what we were going in

68

against. We'd all read plenty about Baxter in the papers—they were the only undefeated 4-A team left in the state—but this was the first chance to watch the fabled juggernaut in action.

Maybe I ought to mention here that things between Dad and me had more or less smoothed out again by this time. I expected a little chilliness out of him following our Friday night flap, but by Saturday afternoon he seemed to have forgotten all about it. And of course I was bending over backward to be nice; it tears me up when Dad gets down on me.

Anyhow, most of us made the scene, and at two o'clock they pulled the shades and Coach Dale started up the projector. What we saw was pretty grim, I don't mind telling you. There are teams that are big and teams that are fast, but in high school ball it's rare to find a team that's both. These boys were. They also had poise, confidence, and the sort of execution that comes from top-notch coaching. These films of course have no sound track, and the room was quiet except for the whirring of the projector, while up there on the screen Baxter High methodically demolished a pretty good group of boys from Colbert County.

When the lights went on again after it was over, there was a lot of scraping of feet and clearing of throats. Skate made some crack about "Godzilla"—meaning McClendon, the monster man—and that brought a rally of nervous laughter.

Dad got up in front of us, smiling and tossing a little piece of chalk.

"How about it, boys? Think you can handle that?"

Somebody in the back said, "I just sprained my ankle, Coach," and that got another big laugh. Even Dad. But then he turned serious again, as he has a way of doing, and the room got quiet.

"I don't know whether we'll beat them or not," he said. "I think we can." He waited a minute to let that sink in. "But it's going to take a better effort than we gave last Friday night. It's going to take eleven guys *wanting* to this time. Eleven guys out there ready to lay it *all* on the line. Do I make myself clear?"

Silence.

"Godzilla," he said, and smiled. That was our cue to laugh again. "I like that, Skate," he said. "Good sobriquet."

Skate was astounded. "Sobriquet? Coach, that baby's mean, drunk *or* sobriquet!" Which of course broke us up again, and Skate, never one to quit while he's winning, went on: "I think he's a racist, man. A Ku Klux Klan."

"But seriously," Dad said, and waited for the room to get quiet. "Seriously—Godzilla, Frankenstein, King Kong, call him anything you like—he's really the bad boy, there's no doubt about that. Last night Coach Dale and myself went over this film at home, and you know what we decided? We decided he's the key. McClendon. This is basically a *defensive* team. Sure, they've run up points against Colbert, against Fairbanks, against Greensboro. But they only do it late in the game when they've beat you on the line. This guy Godzilla will eat your lunch. He'll spit in your eye and tell you it's raining. And do you know how old he is?"

Dead silence this time.

Dad tossed up his little piece of chalk and caught it, letting us wait. (Very effective, I thought, even if he was my dad.)

"He's been driving a car about a year now. The boy's barely seventeen years old."

Before we could oooh and aaah at that, he went on.

"He got that way from milking cows and pitching hay. He's a farm boy."

Skate started to say something funny, but Dad broke in on him.

"No, let me correct that. He's not a boy at all. He's a grown-up man, which is something a lot of people never get to be, even when they're sixty years old and have grandchildren. He's a doggone man-and-a-half, and I wish I had eleven just like him!"

Nobody said anything, not even Skate.

"And he'll eat your lunch and he'll spit in your eye," Dad said again, rubbing it in. "Now I hope I've made it clear that we have Mister McClendon to contend with. I hope I've made it clear that what we'll be facing is a good offense and a *superb* defense. In other words, if we can score, we may be able to win this ball game.

"Coach Dale, if you'll start that film again, I'd like to point out a few things, with special reference to how our friend Godzilla plays the game of football. Teas?"

"Yes, sir."

"Pay close attention now. A lot of this has to do with you."

That passed right over my head at the time—the typical

72

remark you expected him to make—and yet in the end it had so much to do with . . . everything.

After the skull session was over, I made it a point to look for Billy Foxx. I even punched his arm as a friendly gesture.

"Hey, Foxx, need a ride? Going toward the Cave?"

He looked surprised and pleased, but then suddenly his face changed and he shook his head. "Gee, I appreciate it, Pete, but actually I'm not going back quite yet."

"Don't tell me you're doing a few laps around the track."

"Naw, nothing like that." He laughed. He has a shy kind of laugh sometimes. "What it is . . . well, actually I promised somebody I'd give them a hand with their trig—you know, a little tutoring session on the side."

By his using the word "somebody," I knew "somebody" must be a female. It figured. I already told you the girls were turned on to Foxx, and since he didn't date much, a couple of them had hit on schemes like that to lure him out of his shell. He was a good student all right—already tapped for the National Honor Society—but what these gals had in mind wasn't logarithms.

I winked to show him I understood, then gave him a real friendly whack on the rump. It's a tribal custom among young male athletes that if you like somebody, the way to show it is by cuffing him around. Don't ask me why. "I'll give you a rain check," I said. "Take it easy, hear?"

"Thanks, Pete," he said earnestly, looking at me with those Paul Newman eyes. "I really do appreciate it."

This was getting a little sticky—all I'd offered him was a ride to town, and we were both acting as if it was a clutch decision. But there had been some tension between us, and both of us knew it, and this was the peace-pipe scene.

"See you, man."

"So long, Pete."

I cut for my jeep.

It was still too early to go over to Patsy's house, so I went home, crashed on the sofa in the den, and watched the last half of the Jets and the Buffalo Bills. The game was over at four, and then it was either Disneyland or Lucy, so I thought what the heck, maybe I'll go on a little early and see if the Lloyd family is back yet from Grandmother's.

I wish I had waited till five because then I would never have known who "somebody" was.

As I rounded the corner into Willow Street, I saw Billy Foxx leaving Patsy's house.

I never even let up on the gas.

7

Not many things have ever thrown me as hard as that did. It was as if the bottom just fell out of everything. I wasn't only hurt and disappointed; my ego felt as if it had been run over by a truck.

Actually, I went through about three different stages of reaction. First I was just zapped, like a prize fighter that was decked by a punch he never saw coming. Then I made a desperate little defensive rally, running around in my mind looking for logical explanations. Maybe Foxx really did go by to help her with her trig. Maybe they got home early from Grandmother's house. Maybe I was misinterpreting the whole situation.

That didn't last long, however, and then I was down for the count. I knew well enough what kind of trouble Patsy had with trig (she could have given *him* lessons); and besides, if it was all that innocent, why was Foxx so sneaky and secretive about it? Why hadn't he come right out and said "Patsy" instead of "somebody"? For that matter, five would get you ten that nobody went anywhere near "Grandmother's house" the whole afternoon. Patsy didn't want me showing up over there before five because some-one else was coming at three.

My final reaction was somewhat less confused and com-plicated. Simple rage. It really blistered me to think what an ape I'd been. At church they taught you to turn the other cheek. Well, I turned the other cheek all right, and now I had egg on both sides of my face.

I was so mad and so shook up that I didn't even know where I was going—just driving blindly through the streets like a zombie. I don't even know how long I kept it up. But finally I realized it was getting dark, which meant it would soon be suppertime, so I turned around and headed home. Mom met me at the door.

"Where have you been?" she said.

"Patsy's."

Her eyebrows went up in surprise. "If that's the case, she must not have noticed you were there because she's called here for you twice."

"Oh. Well, that was earlier. She must have called since I left."

I started on up the stairs as though I was going to my room to call her back, but I had no intention of calling Patsy Lloyd, not now or later. I was in no mood to discuss it with Mom, either. She had the wind up already. I could tell by the way she looked at me (mothers have an abso-lutely uncanny instinct for that kind of thing), and sooner or later I was going to have to explain. But not now. Now all I wanted was to be left alone to lick my wounds.

Of course the first thing I saw when I went in my room was the big picture of Patsy that I kept on my desk. She

76

was smiling that sweet, deceitful smile of hers, and on a gold chain around her neck was my little gold football. That was something I would have to get back. Also my class ring.

I very politely took the picture and placed it face down in the bottom drawer of my desk. Then I stretched out on my bed and did some more thinking. For a minute I was tempted to call her, just to hear what kind of lies she would make up about how she spent the afternoon. "How was Granny?" I could say, and let her take it from there. But I didn't have the stomach for that either.

Then I began to wonder if maybe she had called up to break me the news—you know, a sort of Dear John via the Bell System. I could imagine her saying something like this: "Pete, this is hard for me to say because you know how I've always felt about you . . . and I hope we can continue being friends . . . but I feel I have to be honest with you. Something very strange and wonderful happened to me at church this morning . . . something over which I have no control . . ."

I've got a real vivid imagination, and that really tore me up, so I quit punishing myself and tried to work up another mad. In a situation of that kind it's better to feel angry than any other way. When you're sore, you're on the offensive, but when you start feeling sorry for yourself, you're just lying there taking a beating.

All at once something hit me out of the blue—something about our phone conversation earlier that afternoon. I got up and ran downstairs to the kitchen, where Mom was fixing dinner.

"Mom, where's the Sunday paper?"

"Which one?"

"The *Times*."

"I think your father's reading it."

I went in the living room and found him with his feet propped up.

"Dad, can I have the paper?"

He looked at me sternly over the top of his glasses. "Sure. When I get through with it."

"Excuse me, I didn't mean to sound rude. I only wanted the section that has the horoscopes in it."

As it turned out, he wasn't reading that section, so he gave it to me and I took it back upstairs.

I hadn't been able to remember the exact wording, but when I found the paragraph, there it was in black and white:

"Scorpio: Recognize end of situation or relationship. Now is time to finish rather than initiate projects. Message will become increasingly clear. Visit one who is confined to home or hospital."

Can you beat that? I mean, did you ever see anything that hit the nail as square on the head?

Recognize end of relationship. Visit one who is confined to home or hospital.

It actually gave me the willies. And was that message ever becoming increasingly clear!

You see, I've always been a great one to scoff at horoscopes and stuff like that. I used to kid Patsy about it. To me it was in the same category as crystal balls and communicating with the dead. But brother, this thing was making a believer out of me.

The next step, naturally, was to have a look at *her* horoscope. Patsy's a Libra. Now get this:

"Libra: Be wary of new alliances. What glitters now may not be gold. Accent is on health and financial matters. Capricorn individual figures prominently in your affairs."

I had no idea when Billy Foxx was born, but at that moment I'd have bet dollars to doughnuts it was between December 22 and January 19. That "financial matters" was a little cloudy (unless it referred to the 8¢ I owed her), but the "accent on health" was clear enough, and even the use of the word "gold," which was an obvious reference to Billy Foxx's blond, curly locks.

Well, it made me feel both good and bad. Bad, because something like this is bound to be out of your hands—you just don't fool around with the stars. But good, because it gave me a little room for hope. In the end things might work out all right, once Pat came to her senses.

But in the meantime, what course was I going to follow? I figured I'd just have to wait for the paper tomorrow morning to find out.

One thing I did, though. That night after Mom and Dad were in bed, I came back downstairs and looked at the gold cup on the mantel—Dad's cup—and I made myself a solemn promise. "Pete," I said, "you're going to win Most Valuable Player."

There was no longer any reason to worry about fairness to Billy Foxx. The guy had been tying me in knots for a month and now was trying to steal my gal. I owed him nothing—except maybe a lump on the head.

"Cool it," I told myself. "Hang loose and concentrate on Number One."

8

"Scorpio: Take time to analyze. Prior commitment should be considered in light of more recent developments. Hold off signing legal documents."

That was my horoscope for Monday morning, and at first I thought somebody was throwing me a curve. I couldn't make head or tail of it. I figured I could hold off signing the legal documents without too much strain, since my average day doesn't include a lot of that sort of thing (if I ever signed one I don't know it), but what was this "prior commitment" they were talking about? Last night I'd made a commitment to myself about winning that cup, but last night isn't very prior. And if there were any developments more recent than that, I didn't know about them yet.

I was still at the breakfast table puzzling over this when Dad left for school (he teaches American History and Drivers Ed), at which point Mom launched the first probe of her investigation into what had happened between Patsy and me. She'd been waiting for him to leave.

"You'd better hurry, Pete, if you plan to go by for Patsy."

Very cunning. She knows I sometimes give Patsy a lift to school. If I said I wasn't picking Patsy up this morning, that would make it possible for her to ask why—a question that would eventually lead us into the gory details. She'd already been in my room that morning and no doubt noticed the picture was missing off my desk. Nothing escapes the eye of a mother.

But I wasn't having any. I just said, "Yeah, I guess so," and put down the paper and started to gather up my books.

"You're not taking a cold, too, are you?"

"No, I don't think so. What made you ask?"

"I don't know," she said. "You look a little peaked."

If I looked a little peaked, it was probably because I dreaded running into Patsy at school. It was going to be awkward facing her now, and I wasn't sure how I was going to handle it. I hate scenes of any kind, and it would have suited me better if I could have avoided her all day and then just gone on avoiding her indefinitely. But of course that wasn't in the cards. No way. For one thing, we had two classes together.

Actually, our big scene didn't take place until after practice, late that afternoon, but there were a couple of stages that led up to it.

Patsy and I have different homerooms, so I didn't really see her till second period when we had English III together. What I did was loiter around the hall until the second bell and then rushed in and took a seat near the door, so I wouldn't have to sit by her. This also enabled me to make a quick getaway when class was over. Out of the corner of my eye I could see her looking at me, but I never even glanced in her direction—except once, and that was to see if she was wearing my gold football. She wasn't. I couldn't tell for sure about the ring because she has one just like it herself; or maybe she was wearing Foxx's by now.

When the bell rang to end the class, I got out of there fast and lost myself in the crowd that was pouring through the halls. I think I heard her call to me, but I pretended not to hear.

This strategy held up pretty good all morning, though there was one time when I saw her coming straight at me down the hall and had to dive in the boys' john. But that afternoon at math class she outsmarted me. I did my tardy student act, rushing into the room at the last minute, only to find Patsy herself occupying the desk next to the door. She had me this time. I was forced to take a seat at the back of the room, and when the class was over, she simply got up and stood there waiting for me. There was no way out, short of climbing through a second-story window.

"Pete?"

"Oh, hi, Pat."

"Are you avoiding me?" She had her books in her arms, clutched to her breast the way girls do, and she was looking up at me with those big, pale brown eyes—a little accusing, but also a little amused, I thought.

"No, I'm not avoiding you," I said, lying in my teeth. "Why should I?"

"That's just what I was wondering myself."

I could feel my face turning red, which is something I've always hated about myself because I have no control over it. Any time anybody looks real hard at me, as though

82

they're confronting me, I feel my stupid face start getting red. This applies mainly to girls and older people, though. Guys my own age don't bother me. I can take on a two-hundred-pound tackle without changing my expression, but let some little hundred-pound female challenge me face to face, and I light up like Old Glory. It's a miserable thing.

"What happened to you yesterday afternoon?" she said.

"To me?"

"Yes, to you. I thought you were coming by."

All at once I forgot about being embarrassed and started to get mad. This was one hell of a note—her standing here to my face, questioning me like I owed *her* some kind of explanation.

"I did come by, Pat," I said coldly. "But when I saw you had company, I decided maybe I ought not to intrude!"

For an instant her face just sort of collapsed. You could tell it really hacked her. Then she gave a little laugh, stalling for time while she thought up an answer.

"Oh, you must mean Billy Foxx," she said.

"I didn't think it was Howard Cosell."

"Oh, so it's *that*," she said, as if we could dismiss the whole subject. "He only dropped by for a minute—wanted to ask me something about a physics problem."

It was physics now instead of trig. Boy, they couldn't even keep their lies straight.

"Pete!"

I had already started to walk away.

"Pete, please don't take that the wrong way. I can explain it, believe me I can. Meet me after school?"

I was still walking, and she was sort of skipping along

beside me. "I've got practice after school," I said. "You know that."

"Then come by tonight."

The bell was ringing for the next class now, and I was moving on out. She could barely keep up.

"Pete, I'll explain the whole silly thing, honest I will. Please come by tonight."

"No."

That word stopped her in her tracks. I went on down the hall and left her where she stood. I knew she was still watching me, but I've no idea what she was thinking. And at that particular moment I didn't care.

Surprisingly, I had a first-rate practice that afternoon. No, it isn't surprising either, because I nearly always play better when I'm a little burned about something. Football is an angry game. But I was careful not to show my emotions, especially to Foxx. In the first place, I didn't want him to know he'd scored a TKO over me; and in the second place, I figured he'd be more vulnerable if he didn't know I had my knife out for him. So I played it cool. He acted friendly, and I did, too—not *overly* friendly or buddy-buddy, just easy and relaxed. Inside, I wasn't at all relaxed; but I put up a good front.

During the first part of the practice the scout team ran Baxter plays against us. Then Dad put Ike Mathis over there in a black scrimmage vest, and we tried running against them. Ike is our right-side linebacker and, as I already pointed out, the biggest guy on the squad. He was acting the part of McClendon, so we started calling him Godzilla, and before long old Ike had his gorge up, too,

and there were some pretty satisfactory licks exchanged. Dad was pleased, Coach Dale was pleased, everybody was pleased—especially me. I knew I was looking good, and I could tell from Dad's manner that he was very encouraged. Maybe in the back of his mind he was beginning to see that gold cup again.

It was a long, hard session and it was strictly football—

by that I mean there was no time to think of anything else. Patsy was completely out of my mind for two and a half hours. As soon as it was over, though, the roof fell in again. We were in the showers, and Skate and Teas were horsing around, snapping wet towels at everybody. I was so touchy that it made me sore. Then Foxx came in with his shampoo and started washing his hair. He's very proud of that blond hair of his, and he shampoos it after every practice. "What glitters now may not be gold," I said to myself, remembering Pat's horoscope. Then I thought of that other line: "Capricorn individual figures prominently in your affairs."

"Hey, Billy," I said. "When were you born?"

"Me?" He wiped the lather back and looked at me with those Paul Newmans. "In 1954."

"No, I mean what month and date."

"November 24."

"Really? I thought you were a Capricorn individual."

"No, Sagittarius. Why?"

"Just checking up."

Somebody popped me with a towel from behind, and said: "I'm a Capricorn. What about it?"

It was Jack Teas.

I was still mulling that one over when I went out to my jeep . . . and found Patsy sitting in it with her school books in her lap.

"For Pete's sake, Patsy! You been waiting here all this time?"

"No, for Pat's sake," she said, and gave me one of those

86

wistful little smiles that makes you think it must have been practiced in front of a mirror.

I'll have to admit it threw me for a minute; I hadn't expected her to be this determined. But then I remembered to be sore. "Aren't you afraid Foxx will see us together?"

"Pete, will you please cut that out. I didn't wait out here for two and a half hours to get barked at."

"Then why did you wait?"

"Because you seem to have gotten some stupid idea in your head about me and Billy Foxx, and I want to make you see how wrong you are."

"Let's start with Grandmother," I said. "Am I wrong in thinking you said you were going to visit your grandmother Sunday afternoon?"

"No, that's what I told you."

"Am I wrong in thinking you didn't go?"

"No, you're right, we didn't."

"Am I wrong in thinking there was never any intention of going to Grandmother's? That you only told me that to keep me from coming straight over after practice?"

"I'll admit that, too."

"And am I wrong in thinking the reason you didn't want me over there was because Billy Foxx was coming? You made the date at church that morning—am I wrong yet?"

"Pete, I willingly admit that everything you've said up to now is true, and I'm also willing to admit that you have a right to your suspicions. I'm sure it must have looked very odd to you, but . . ."

"Odd? Nothing odd about it. I've seen it happen to any

number of guys. I mean, I may be dumb, but I'm not crazy."

"Pete, you just don't understand. It wasn't at all like what you think. Actually, Billy didn't come because of *me*."

"So now he's got a crush on your mother? Aw, come on, Pat."

"Will you shut up and listen? I'm trying to tell you I have no interest in Billy Foxx and he has none in me. He only came to my house because . . . well, it was another matter entirely."

"What?"

"I already told you."

"Tell me again."

"He was having trouble with a physics problem."

"Now, that *is* odd," I said. "Because he told me he was going to help somebody with their *trig*."

That was the clincher; it really hacked her. I saw her bite her lip, and for a minute I thought she was going to cry.

"Pete, please try to understand. I'd explain the whole thing in detail if I could, but I just can't!"

"No, of course you can't. 'Oh, what a tangled web we weave when first we practice to deceive.' " That was a little corny, me quoting from Shakespeare and all, but this was the Big Scene, and I figured I might as well pull out all the stops.

"Can't you just take my word for it? Can't you just trust me?"

"You know, the only thing that really puzzles me is why you want to bother stringing me along, now that you've got Foxx."

88

She dropped her face in her hands, and when she looked up again, there were tears in her eyes; but she seemed more angry than anything else.

"You know what's wrong with you?" she said. "You're obsessed with Billy Foxx. You're so insanely jealous of him, you're willing to believe anything about him, just so it's bad. I think you need to see a psychiatrist!"

That did it. Now she was telling me I was crazy. "Are you ready for me to take you home?"

"Don't bother," she said. "I'll walk."

The next day at school Kitty Bell, who is probably Patsy's closest friend, handed me a little box she had been asked to deliver. I didn't have to open it to know what was inside: my ring and my gold football. Rock bottom.

No, not quite. Rock bottom was yet to come.

9

Tuesday and Wednesday just sort of drifted by in a haze. At school Patsy and I passed each other in the halls like a couple of sleepwalkers, eyes glassy and straight ahead, neither of us willing to notice the other was alive. Both Kitty and Angy came to me and dropped hints the size of watermelons about how unhappy "a certain person" was and how the dance wasn't going to be much fun since "not everybody" would be there. I turned them all a deaf ear. Let Foxx take her to the dance.

I think it was on Wednesday that Mom finally abandoned her subtle tactics and made the frontal assault.

"Pete, I want to know what's happened between you and Patsy. I've been hearing all sorts of wild rumors."

"It's true. We've busted up, Mom."

"Well, I'm certainly distressed to hear it. I think Patsy's an adorable girl, and I can't imagine what it's all about."

"Try imagining a tall, good-looking guy with blond hair and blue eyes, and make him a big star on the football team."

"I'm aware that Billy Foxx called on Patsy last Sunday afternoon," she said, "but according to her mother, it was not in the nature of a social call. And furthermore, he has not been to see her since."

"Maybe not to her house, but I've seen them whispering together several times, and once *behind* the gymnasium."

"Since Sunday?"

"Since Sunday."

I'll admit it puzzled me a little at first why Patsy kept trying to deny her interest in Foxx—and kept sending out her tenacles toward me—but I finally figured it out. You see, the Lloyds are upper-crust society folks, whereas Billy Foxx's mother is only a forelady at the hosiery mill. In other words, it was a little embarrassing for the stuck-up Lloyds to have their daughter linked romantically with a boy of such low station, even if he was a football hero. I could imagine they were putting quite a lot of pressure on Patsy about it. Then there was also the ego thing. Patsy hadn't dropped me; *I* had dropped *her*. You have to know the workings of the female mind to understand these things. But even if Patsy really was sorry and really did wish we hadn't broken up, the fact remained that on at least one occasion she had deliberately lied to me and deceived me. I didn't think I could ever feel quite the same toward her again.

Women are peculiar creatures, but in the same breath I have to say men are, too. Take my dad, for instance. During all this hullabaloo about me and Patsy and Billy Foxx, he never noticed a thing was wrong. Completely oblivious to the whole affair. While I trooped around the house as gloomy as Hamlet, Dad went around humming, whistling, feeling great. All he had on his mind was football, and it so happened that during this time the football was going well, so he was happy. If anybody had said to him, "What's wrong with Pete? Why does he look so down-in-the-mouth?" I'm sure Dad would have been very surprised at the question. "Pete? Why, Pete's fine! Didn't you see him run the option at scrimmage today?"

One night I even caught him moving his trophies around on the mantel, as though he were seeing if there was room up there for another one. That brought it back to me how much—how *really* much—he wanted me to win that award. And right there I recommitted myself, if there is such a word.

As I say, Tuesday and Wednesday just sort of drifted by in a haze. I'd come home from practice completely bushed but still too restless to want to stay home, and yet if I went to the Cave or to a show, there was always the risk of running into Patsy or Billy Foxx—or worse, running into both of them together. On the scrimmage field I didn't mind working with Foxx too much; he was strictly business out there, the same as I was. But if I'd met him somewhere like at the Cave, I honestly don't know what I would have said to him. I guess I would have just turned red in the face, like a moron.

"Hey, man," Skate said to me, "what happened with you and your chick?"

"It just wasn't in the stars, Skate."

Speaking of stars, there's one thing I've noticed about horoscopes—they never really give you any bad news. Have you ever noticed that? Either they're faking it, or there are times when they just don't have the heart to tell you. They give little gentle warnings from time to time like, "Accent is on health," or "Be wary of new alliances," and "Hold off signing legal documents." But where did you ever see one that said, "Don't go near the water," or "Whatever you do, don't drive a car today." I mean, people get drowned and people have car wrecks all the time, and it seems to me a lot of that could be avoided if the guy that figures out the horoscopes would be a little more specific and stop beating around the bush. Where did you ever see a horoscope that came right out and said: "Boy, are you going to catch it today!" Or, "If you haven't yet made a will, be sure to do so before three o'clock this afternoon!"

What I'm leading up to is my horoscope Thursday morning in the *Times,* which went like this:

"Scorpio: Don't be startled in regard to message associated with relative. What appears serious now may turn out better in the end. Unexpected surprises are in store."

In view of what was really in store for me Thursday, that could hardly be considered a legitimate piece of journalism.

What my Thursday horoscope should have said was something like this: "Bad news in store for you in regard to friends *and* relative. Get set for rock bottom, buddy-boy."

On the Thursday before a Friday game, we don't ordinarily dress out in pads. It's not a good idea to do any contact work that close to game time because of the possibility of injuries. As a usual thing, we go through our drills in shorts or sweats. It didn't surprise me, then, to see Dad still in his street clothes when I arrived at the dressing room that afternoon. But what did surprise me was to see that none of the players had changed either. I was a little late and the room was half full when I got there—guys just sitting around in sweaters and jackets, as though practice had been called off for the day.

It was awful quiet in that room, too, I noticed. Everybody was glancing around, looking sort of puzzled and uneasy.

"What gives?" I said.

"Sit down, Pete," Dad said. He didn't say another word, but the look on his face told me something was wrong. He looked like the executioner about to execute. Grim was hardly the word for it. Morose, maybe. He was leaning against the edge of one of the massage tables with his arms folded over his chest, and trailing down from one hand was a long, narrow piece of paper. Having worked on the school newspaper, I recognized what it was right away. It was a galley proof.

A few more guys straggled in, looked surprised at what was going on, and took their places silently.

"That everybody, Coach?" Dad asked.

"I believe so," said Dale.

"How about locking the door for a few minutes."

That really sounded ominous. All at once I felt scared, and I didn't know why.

"First, let me say that practice is canceled today. After I get through with what I have to say, I want all of you to go home and take it easy. Go to bed early and get a good night's sleep. I think we're as ready for Baxter as we'll ever be, and the rest will do you more good than another workout.

94

"I'd also like to say that I'm very pleased with the way we've worked this week. You boys have shown a lot of character, and I'm proud of you. That's what makes it so hard for me to say what I have to say next."

He unfolded his arms and held up that long, narrow strip of newsprint. "This right here is a copy of Quinton Winters' sports column, which is scheduled to appear in tomorrow's *Gazette*. Never mind how I happened to get my hands on it —let's just say we have friends, as well as enemies, at the *Gazette*. Most of it has to do with our chances of beating Baxter tomorrow night—which are pretty slim according to Mr. Winters—so I'm not going to read all of it to you. Mr. Winters' judgments are not of the least importance to me at this point. However, there's one paragraph that does concern me deeply, and that one I am going to read. Here it is:

" 'Another thing that makes us doubtful is the attitude of some of the players. To cite an example, last Saturday night three members of the squad were seen celebrating the Greensboro victory with a beer party at the 500 Club in Elkton. In deference to the rest of the team, and the coaching staff, we refrain from naming names; but it does seem to us the sort of thing that might have a deleterious effect on the squad as a whole, not to say what it does to the image of the school. Drunkenness is never pretty, and in a teen-age boy it is both deplorable and distressing.' "

I looked across the room at Teas, and his face was white as chalk. I guess mine was, too. At this point I was still too stunned to even be angry.

"Boys," Dad went on, "in all my years of coaching, I

think this is the most disappointing thing that's ever happened.

"Now, we have rules, and we all know those rules. And like it or not, Mr. Winters is correct in saying that we also have the school's image to think of. We cannot tolerate this kind of behavior."

He took a deep breath and then went on.

"I don't know who those three boys are, and I wish I didn't ever have to know. But as head football coach, it is my obligation to take action in response to these charges. I earnestly hope that those three, whoever they are, will be honorable enough to face *their* obligation to the team and the school.

"Tomorrow morning at eight o'clock I'll be here in the equipment room. I expect those three boys to come to me and turn in their uniforms."

10

I went out of there like a zombie in a state of deep shock. "No," I thought, "it can't be true. I'm dreaming. It's a nightmare."

All around me there was a rumble, too, coming from the other guys on the squad. They were plenty sore, and I don't blame them at all. They themselves had done nothing wrong, and to have something like this hit them right before the biggest game of the year . . . it just wasn't fair. Everybody was throwing suspicious looks at everybody else, while the team spirit and the old battle morale went up in blue smoke. But at that moment I was too sunk in my own private misery to care what they were saying or what they were thinking. I felt as though my world had come to an end; as though the stars had ganged up on me and decided to finish me off once and for all. Running away from home would almost have been a better outlook than having to go in there tomorrow and see the expression on Dad's face when he found out I was one of the three. It was going to kill my dad—I mean absolutely destroy the guy. Talk about winning the Most Valuable Player award—I was going to win the honky-tonk award! Of course I knew I wasn't guilty of all the things Winters was saying in that column of his, but at the same time it was a weak case I had to plead. The lawyers have a phrase for it, don't they—guilty by association? I'd broken the training rules (and probably the law, too) by going in a place where liquor was served, and I had not opened my mouth to object when Teas ordered the beer. Beer had been on the table there in front of all of us, and anybody who saw us might have assumed the very things Winters was suggesting. No matter how you sliced it, there was no denying the fact that our presence at the 500 Club did nothing to improve the image of the school. But me, big stupe, I never gave that a thought at the time. Looking back on it now and in this light, I must have been out of my mind to ever step foot in the place. Maybe Patsy was right—I did need a shrink. The pressure had addled my brain.

I'd got as far as the parking lot, almost to my jeep, when somebody grabbed me by the arm.

"I'll kill him! I'll break every bone in his body!"

It was Dave Stone, looking like a wild man and breathing as if he'd just run a four-forty.

"Now, don't start blaming it all on Jack," I said. "We both went along. We both . . ."

"I'm not talking about Jack," he said. "I'm talking about that low-life, rotten S.O.B. Quinton Winters. Pete, we weren't drunk, for crying out loud. Me and you never touched a thing stronger than a Coke!"

"I know, I know. Listen, get in the car before somebody hears you."

We both crawled in the jeep, and he sat there breathing through his nose like a big white-faced bull about to charge. "I tell you, Pete, if I miss the Baxter game because of that lying, rotten S.O.B . . ."

"You're beginning to repeat yourself, Dave," I said. "Let's be calm for a minute and try to think. Jumping on Quinton Winters isn't going to change anything now."

"I'll change his face," he said. The idea seemed to please him, and he went on, "I'll change his hat size with the lumps I put on his head."

He raved on for a while, and I let him, but finally he ran out of steam and sank into a gloomy, dejected mood like me.

"Pete, what on earth are we going to do? You realize what happens if you and I and Jack don't play? Baxter will slaughter us. The score'll be a hundred to nothing. Who's he got left to put in the game?"

"Edmonds for Teas. Milton at quarterback . . ."

"Milton at quarterback?" He was astounded. "Dickey Milton? A sophomore that hasn't played four quarters all season?"

"The kid has a lot of ability. He can throw the ball as well as I can right now."

"Dickey Milton?"

"And at fullback he can use . . ."

"They'll kill him. That Godzilla character will make oatmeal out of him."

I quit trying to argue because he was right of course. I'm not bragging, just being realistic. Without the three of us in the game, there was no backfield left, only Billy Foxx. And

100

good as he was, Foxx couldn't go it alone. But here's a funny thing: while Dave was thinking only of the team, I was thinking of my dad. All at once I could see him out there, pacing the sidelines in his overcoat, trying to make the best of it—getting slaughtered. Getting humiliated because three stupid guys didn't have sense enough to keep their nose clean for one more week.

"We blew it, Dave."

"Yeah," he said miserably, "I guess we did in a way. But I never dreamed of anything like this happening. Why would a guy—even a guy as rotten as Quint Winters—want to sandbag his own team like that?"

"His own *school,*" I corrected. "He never played on the team, remember?"

"Maybe that's part of the reason. Maybe he's jealous or something."

"And then of course I had to go and rub his nose in it. If I hadn't teed him off over there that night, none of this would have happened."

Dave said nothing, which meant that he agreed.

"It's wrong to knock a guy for not playing ball. Some people just aren't cut out for it, and they can't help it. I never should have laid that on him."

"Still, it was a rotten thing to do. At least he could have told the truth. And who'd have thought your dad would take such a strong stand on it?"

"He doesn't know who the three guys are yet," I said. "Maybe he thinks it's three deadheads off the bench and he'll never miss them."

"Cut it out, Pete. You know your dad better than that.

He'd be just as hurt and just as disappointed if it turned out to be the water boy."

This time it was my turn to say nothing because Dave was right about that, too. To Dad the squad was like a family; what any one of us did reflected on all the others, including him. I've seen him get just as upset over a third-string guard who was flunking his grades as a guy in the starting lineup.

"So what do we do?" Dave said. "Do we creep in there tomorrow with our tail between our legs and turn in our jocks? I'm not willing to do that, Pete. I just don't feel that guilty. Sure, we had our head up and locked when we went to the 500, but was it really all that bad? Maybe if all three of us went in there and told him the truth, really shelled the corn, maybe he'd have a change of heart. I mean, I hate to see that Coke I drank cost me the Baxter game."

"Dad's not famous for his changes of heart. Usually when he takes a stand on something, that's it."

"Well, maybe we could at least persuade him to let *you* play. They can get by without me, and they might get by without Teas, but without a quarterback we're dead sunk, Pete."

"Thanks, Dave. But you're forgetting one thing, aren't you?"

"What?"

"Jack didn't drink a Coke."

He frowned as he thought about it. "Yeah, I see what you mean. There's no way out for Jack, is there? It would be like throwing him to the wolves if we did that."

"And how good a friend are you to Jack?"

He nodded slowly; then suddenly he sat straight up in the seat. "By the way," he said, "where *is* Jack? Why isn't he out here helping us sweat this out?"

All at once I had another of my revelations, sort of like the one I had in church Sunday morning. I looked around the parking lot, and sure enough, everyone had gone. There wasn't a car left except my old heap—and one other. A powder-blue Camaro was still parked by the dressing-room door.

"Dave," I said, "knowing the spot we're in and how we got there, where would you expect Jack Teas to be right now?"

"Huh?"

"Take a look over your shoulder."

He craned his big size 17 neck around, and when he saw the car by the dressing-room door, he tensed a little and then relaxed.

"I'll be doggone," he said. "I ought to have my tail kicked for what I was thinking."

"He's a beautiful guy, isn't he? I hope he's a good talker."

It was five o'clock when Dad finally came home. I'd been waiting and watching for him since four, and by the time he turned in at the gate, I had finished chewing my finger-nails and was starting on the quick. He was walking briskly, I noticed, and he was whistling—pretty good sign. I had the door open before he got to the porch.

"Well, Dad?"

He looked up, surprised. "Well what?"

"Teas," I said. "What did he tell you?"

"Oh, so you noticed he stayed after the others left."

"Yes, Dave and I were in the parking lot."

"Well, it was good news and bad, Pete. Let me get a cup of coffee and I'll tell you where we stand."

Feeling a little confused, not to say apprehensive, I watched him hang up his coat and hat and then followed him into the kitchen. Luckily, Mom was not there. Up to now his expression told me nothing. He looked serious, maybe even a little grim, but it wasn't the face of a man who has been crushed with disillusionment.

He took his time with the coffee, the way they build up suspense in one of those Alfred Hitchcock movies. He tasted it, frowned, stirred in some more sugar, and tasted it again.

"Your mother makes the worst coffee in town," he said.

I wanted to yell, "Come on, what happened?" but instead I just stood there and privately broke a sweat.

"I don't know what it is," he said, "whether she puts in too much water or not enough coffee."

"Dad. What happened with Teas?"

He took a deep breath, then let it all out at once, the way people do when they've stalled as long as they can and now it's time to face something unpleasant.

"Jack won't be playing tomorrow night, Pete. He turned in his suit."

I swallowed. "He told you the whole story then."

"Yes, and he showed a lot of courage about it, too, a lot of character. I like the way he came right out with it, didn't hesitate or equivocate. Walked right up and admitted he was guilty."

Dad seemed to be looking at me pretty intently as he said that. It was all I could do to look back at him.

"Jack's a fine boy," he went on, "guilty of nothing more than indiscretion, and I hate like the devil to cut him from the squad right now, just before the big game of his senior year. But under the circumstances I had no choice about it. We make certain rules, we draw certain lines, and we do so in the best interest of everybody. The rules *apply* to everybody. It wouldn't be fair to the boys who play it straight to start making exceptions for those who don't. If we did, pretty soon there'd be no rules at all and the whole thing would fall apart. Do you agree with me, Pete?"

He made it a point to look right in my eyes when he said that, and this time I really felt my hopes sink.

"Yes, sir, I agree," I said humbly.

"The true facts, however, are not quite as damaging as Mr. Winters would have us believe. As a matter of actual fact, most of his allegations are maliciously false—I might even go so far as to say they are outright damn lies! Jack swears that of the three boys, he was the only one who drank any beer at all. He gave me his word of honor this afternoon that neither of the other two boys touched anything stronger than Coke."

"Wait a minute," I said. "The other two boys . . . ?"

"He wouldn't tell me their names, and I didn't press him. He was conducting himself like a gentleman, and I respected him for it. Besides, this puts a whole new complexion on the thing. I'm not going to kick anybody off the team for drinking a Coke—even though he did pick a bad place to drink it."

All at once a lump the size of a hen egg came up in my throat. Good old Teas—still in there pitching, still trying to salvage what he could for me and Dave, for the team and the school, even though he himself was going down like the Red Baron.

"Dad . . ."

"Another thing. He didn't beg or plead or try to get me to change my decision, just laid it right on the line and said he hoped I'd reconsider the case of the other two boys. As a matter of fact, he took all the blame on himself—said he persuaded them to go with him to the club when they really didn't want to go in the first place."

"Dad . . ."

"So as far as I'm concerned, the incident is closed. I'm sorry about Jack, and not having him on the field is going to hurt us; but it's to his credit that he behaved like a man about it."

"Dad, will you please let me say a few words? About those other two guys? Listen, I admire Jack for what he is trying to do, but I can't hold still for it. I have to tell you I was one of them myself."

There was real surprise in his eyes for an instant, and maybe a little shadow of disappointment. But then a wry kind of grin pulled up one corner of his mouth, and he said: "Well, that completes the trio. Dave Stone waylaid me on the way home and made his confession. Everybody seems to want to get in this act."

I didn't know what to say, so I kept my mouth shut.

He took another sip of his coffee and gazed thoughtfully out the window. "You know, Pete, as you grow older, you'll learn a lot of things, and one of them is this: sometimes life will punish you just as hard for an innocent mistake as it will for a deliberate transgression. In this instance you've been lucky. Bear that in mind."

"Yes, sir."

As I turned to leave the kitchen, he called to me again. "Pete."

"Yes, sir?"

"Thanks, son."

I had hardly closed the door of my room before there was a light knock, and Mom looked in.

"Can I intrude?"

"Sure, Mom, come on in."

She sat down on the bed beside me and put an arm around my shoulder. "Pete," she said, "if I ask you something personal, will you promise to give me a completely honest, forthright answer?"

"Well, yes. I seem to be on that kick today." What, I wondered, is coming next?

"Do I really make the worst coffee in town?"

I looked at her and suddenly laughed out loud. "Mom, you rat, you were listening all the time!"

"Me an eavesdropper?" She pretended to be shocked. "Can I help it if that's a louvred door between the kitchen and the laundry room?"

"Poor Dad. He'd die if he knew you heard him say that."

She laughed gaily, but then just as quickly turned serious again. She can do that, and it's a quality that makes her still seem young to me, girlish almost.

"Your father's feeling a little humble about all this himself," she said.

"Why him?"

"Because he suspected Billy Foxx instead of his own son."

"You mean . . ."

She was already nodding her head. "He's a little ashamed of his selfish motivation, or whatever it was. He knows now that subconsciously he *wanted* it to be Billy Foxx."

"He told you this?"

"In a roundabout way. He tells me everything."

"Except the truth about your coffee."

She made a tiny fist and punched the air in front of my chin. "I gotta get out of here and put some supper on the table, kid."

"Mom." I stopped her before she reached the door. "Now that I've been honest and forthright with you, how about your doing the same for me. One question."

"This may not get you any brownie points," she warned.

"Did you suspect that I was one of the bad guys in this boozy melodrama?"

"I knew you were, Pete. That's what made it so bad when I realized what your father was thinking."

"But how could you have known?"

"Remember the rubber stamp on the back of your hand? That stuff is hard to wash off, and it was still on there at church Sunday morning. I noticed it during Communion."

"Hey, but how'd you know what it meant?"

She laughed gaily again. "I was young myself once, egghead!" And before I could say anything else, she swung the door wide and did one of those Loretta Young exits with her skirt swirling.

Later that night at supper I said to Dad: "Didn't it ever occur to you that Jack Teas might be lying?"

"Nope," he said, over a forkful of spaghetti. "Not even for a minute."

11

Friday I was very careful not to read my horoscope in the morning paper. I had enough on my mind without being bugged with a lot of riddles from outer space. Besides, I had reached the place where I figured it was time to throw over astrology in favor of a little positive thinking. There's two schools of thought, as I understand it. Some people—namely the horoscope readers—seem to believe that everything that happens to you is predestined or preordained, and there's not much you can do about it except brace yourself. The other school—the positive thinkers— say it's all in your head. If you *believe* you can do something, you can. Anything you believe strong enough becomes a reality. I'm not sure either of them really has the final answer nailed down. Astrology has a lot of holes in it from the point of view of logic; and there's got to be a limit to how far just believing something will get you. For example, if I started out believing I was Napoleon Bonaparte, they've got a place for folks like that. But as of Friday morning I was leaning more toward the positive thinkers

110

than the stargazers—in other words, I was taking matters into my own hands for a change. If somebody had come along with a legal document, I probably would have gone ahead and signed it.

One thing I did read, though, was Quinton Winters' column in the *Gazette*. To my surprise, the paragraph about the three drunks at the 500 Club was nowhere in it. I guess at the last minute Quinton's conscience got to bothering him—or his better judgment—and he deleted it before they went to press. But how was that for irony? Most of the damage was already done; Teas was out of the lineup.

As I say, I didn't look at my horoscope, but if it was anywhere near accurate, it must have said something to the effect that this was going to be the longest day of my life. The weather was perfect—clear and crisp and bright gold —and that somehow heightened the feeling of excited tension that was running through the whole school. It was almost like an electric current that somebody was turning gradually higher and higher with a voltage regulator. You could feel the suspense mounting as the hours crawled by toward game time. Everybody was talking loud and laughing a lot, and the teachers finally gave up trying to be serious about the class work and got caught up in the carnival mood themselves. All along the halls there were signs and posters proclaiming how bad we were going to beat Baxter, and every guy that played on the squad became an instant celebrity. People were clapping you on the back and yelling "good luck"—some of them people that didn't ordinarily bother to say hello. There had been a pep rally and bonfire the night before, but during the noon break for lunch another one started up spontaneously in the quadrangle and ended in a gigantic snake dance that went all the way through the east-west corridor of the school and lasted till after the tardy bell. From time to time I kept catching glimpses of Patsy, and she seemed as happy and excited as everyone else. In fact, at one point during the snake dance Billy Foxx was marching right behind her with his hands on her hips. I wasn't close enough to tell if she was wearing his ring or not, but I told myself it didn't matter.

During all this, Jack Teas was slinking around the school avoiding all of us like a fugitive from justice. Finally Dave and I put the clamps on him.

"Remember us? We used to kid around together."

"Aw, cut it out, you guys," Teas said, hanging his head. "I blew it for everybody, and the whole school knows it."

"Yeah," I said, "but does the whole school know you took all the blame on yourself so Dave and I could play?"

He shrugged miserably. "What difference does that make if we lose?"

Dave cuffed him roughly on the shoulder. "Come on, Jack, you're dragging your tracks out with the seat of your pants. We're kinda proud of you for what you did. Right, Pete?"

"Absolutely."

He looked up, and a smile of relief broke over his face. "Thanks, guys."

"No," I said, "we're here to thank you."

Football didn't really officially begin until six o'clock that evening when we filed tensely into the locker room and

112

started to get taped and dressed. Usually at this point before a game I can relax a little; it's as though things have finally been put in motion and you're riding that crest that carries you through the kickoff and into the sudden, explosive relief that comes with the first action. But tonight I wasn't getting that feeling. The tension was still building, and no matter how many times I dried my palms, they still seemed to be wet.

By now of course everybody knew about Teas, and that put a damper on things. Even Skate was tense and quiet. But outside, the stadium parking lot was beginning to fill up, and the sound of cars and people and excitement had started to grow. From the window we saw two big Greyhound buses rock through the gate, bringing the Baxter team, and that was the only time Skate said anything funny at all.

"They got the team in one bus and Godzilla in the other," he said. "The one with the bars on the windows."

Cars were shooting back and forth in the street, dragging long streamers of orange crepe paper, and most of them had stuff like "Beat Baxter" painted on the doors with water paint. You have to stand on a bench to see out our locker-room windows, and just before I got down to finish dressing, little Mel Edmonds climbed up beside me. He's so short that he couldn't see out, even with his cleats on.

"What's going on out there, Pete?" he said.

"Nothing special. Just the crowd arriving." Actually, when he asked me that, I was watching the ambulance crawl through the gate like a big sinister gray cat. I figured it was just as well Mel didn't see it. Playing Teas's position

113

tonight, he'd have to contend with Mister McClendon more than anyone else, and at a hundred and thirty-five pounds, he'd be lucky not to get hurt.

At a quarter to seven we went out for our warm-up, and a few minutes later Baxter came on the field and we had our first good look at the guy we were calling Godzilla. It wasn't hard to spot him, even though he was not the biggest guy on their squad by any means. They had an end and a tackle that were both bigger and taller, and another kid who might have been a back—I wasn't sure. But what made it funny, this McClendon character actually did look a lot like an ape. He was stubby from his waist down, but he had one of those short, thick necks, big shoulders, and arms that hung down nearly to his knees. Those meat hooks of his stretched about a foot out of the sleeves of his jersey. Baxter wears a black-and-red uniform that is mostly black with red numbers and red piping, and under that black helmet with the cage over his face, this McClendon was an evil-looking piece of plunder, I don't mind telling you. It wasn't possible to see his face at all, and that made it worse—as if he really were a monster out there in a football suit.

We went through our quicks and stretches, and then Dickey Milton and I threw passes to the backs and ends while the interior linemen went through some drills under Coach Dale. Next came punting, then play-running, and before I knew it, it was time to go back in for the soul session. The stadium was full to overflowing now, and the crowd noise was a constant, steady surflike sound coming at us from both sides. Now and then I could hear Foxx's

114

name called out, but I didn't let it bother me. Just as we crossed the track and went through the gate at the end of the field, I looked up and saw a big orange harvest moon balanced on top of the east stands' press box. "That's good luck," I thought, "because orange is our color." All at once I felt a lot better. The physical activity had calmed my nerves, and my body felt tight and compact, the way it ought to feel when you're tuned and ready to play ball. Maybe—just maybe—I was going to have my best game ever.

Back in the dressing room they gave each of us a little cup of fruit juice, and we sat down to hear what Dad had to say.

"There's not a lot to remember about this team," he said. "They play a fairly simple brand of football, as all of you should know by now. They come right at you, and they keep on coming. But it's mainly their defense that wins ball games for them, and I think if we can put some points on the board, we have a very good chance of beating them. They're not used to having people move the ball on them, and who knows, it just might destroy their poise when we start doing it. We'll be running the option quite a bit tonight, and we hope to be able to get the ball to Foxx, outside. Mel? Where is Mel Edmonds?"

"Right here, Coach." Mel raised his hand.

Dad opened his mouth to say something, then checked himself and smiled. "Well, David, you're in the lions' den to-night."

Everybody laughed at that, and little Mel turned red.

"Well, don't you guys worry about Mel Edmonds," Dad

said. "He's small, but I wish all of you had his kind of guts. I'm not worried about Mel Edmonds. But I do want to say this to you, Mel. This McClendon boy is an all-state linebacker, and he didn't get that from being soft and sloppy. He's going to beat you plenty out there tonight. I expect that. But the important thing is *don't give up*. If he beats you nine times out of ten, that tenth time, when you beat him, just might be the time that wins the game for us. You understand? We only need a few breaks—maybe only one —so just keep playing him the best you know how, and keep watching for that time when he gets careless or lets up a little. Do I make myself clear?"

Mel nodded. His jaw was set and his face was pale—a Kamikaze.

"One other thing. Pete?"

"Yes, sir."

"If they start stunting on the weak side, remember your Pass Nine Sprint-out. Also the draw." Suddenly he looked up, straight at me. "The *tailback* draw."

"Yes, sir."

"Coach Dale, do you have anything you'd like to add to this?"

Dale shook his head.

"One last thing," Dad said. "There's a face missing here tonight. I don't want to go into all the details and ramifications of it now—you probably know anyhow. But I would like to say that everything has worked out for the best, and regardless of how this game comes out, I think I'll be as proud of Jack Teas as any of you who play tonight."

There was a moment of choked, emotional silence.

"Game captains will be Ike Mathis and Mel Edmonds."

Everybody applauded, and Mel turned red again.

"Now what do you say?"

We scrambled to our feet, and fifty-two voices let go a rebel yell.

"I couldn't hear you."

We yelled again.

"Still can't hear you!"

That time we all but cracked the plaster.

Dad grinned with satisfaction. His eyes were bright as a kid's with excitement, and I thought to myself: *He's remembering it now, reliving it all again, twenty-nine years ago, his own finest game.*

"All right, let's go get 'em!"

As we ran onto the field, six thousand people rose as one man, and when the roar hit us, it was like breasting a wave.

12

Ike and Mel walked out to meet the Baxter captains at midfield looking like Mutt and Jeff—Ike six feet tall and two thirty-five; Mel five feet six and *one* thirty-five. The crowd was about as keyed up as the players, and a little ripple of nervous laughter ran through the stands.

We won the toss and elected to receive; there was no wind worth mentioning.

The pastor of the Methodist Church said the invocation over the loudspeaker while we all stood with our heads bowed, holding our helmets in our hands and thinking about everything on earth except what he was saying. Then the boys from the ROTC unit ran the flag up as the band played the National Anthem. Finally it was game time.

Although Skate's an end, we usually put him back with the deep men on kickoffs because he's fast and has good hands. The fans on our side of the field, all standing now, were hoping Foxx would be the receiver; but evidently Baxter had heard about Billy Foxx, and they were careful to boot the ball away from him to the other side.

Skate caught it about two yards deep in the end zone and came right up the middle. He managed to get out nearly to the twenty, though I don't know how. It seemed like the whole Baxter team arrived with the ball, and when they hemmed old Skate up and started to nail him down, you could have heard the pads popping in the next county. These guys actually ran over each other to get a lick in. I was surprised Skate was able to get up.

The first play from scrimmage is one play every quarterback dreads, especially when you're deep in your own territory, which you usually are. It's almost a wasted down, really, because all you're concentrating on is not fumbling. Everybody's so tight that there's a great temptation to call something safe and simple, not expecting any yardage, just a release of the tension. And normally that's exactly what I would have done.

But not tonight. Tonight I had made up my mind to come out with both guns blazing. It was my last game for Morgan, and there was too much riding on the outcome for me to pussyfoot around. Positive Pete was going for broke.

"Right, Formation One, Pass Seven, X Circle!"

"Pass?" It came out a single word, spoken in one voice by about half the guys in the huddle, as if they had rehearsed it.

"Why don't you fellows repeat that a little louder?" I said. "I don't believe that Baxter safety man heard you."

"Sure, airmail it, daddy!" That was Skate of course. He likes it wild and wooly.

"On first sound," I said, not giving anybody a chance to object, and we broke the huddle.

As it turned out, Bart Starr couldn't have called a better play. It must have been an inspiration. Baxter, being a team that plays a conservative game, apparently had gotten in the habit of thinking conservatively.

Jake Grider, our split end, caught the ball on his finger-tips crossing behind the linebackers, and for a minute I swear I thought he was going all the way. When they finally hauled him down, we were on their side of the fifty by three yards. Talk about a crowd going wild! Against the number one team in the state, our first play had carried thirty-three yards, and we were already camped in their territory.

I knew this had them a little rattled, so now was the time to throw the Sunday punch. Triple option.

"Right, Formation One, Eleven Option!"

It was on this particular play that I got personally acquainted with Mister Godzilla. I faked the ball to Stone, who plowed into the line like a howitzer round, and then I was running west behind the line with Foxx in the corner of my eye, watching to see what the end would do. The end kept fading, playing Foxx for the pitch, so when I had gone far enough to open a gap between him and his tackle, I tucked the ball under my arm and made a hard left turn. For an instant it looked good, as though I had maybe six or eight yards. But then something big and black loomed up in the gap. All I remember seeing was a white mouthpiece grinning at me through a cage. He didn't break down and drive his helmet into my numbers like most linebackers do; he just spread those big arms in a loving embrace and met me standing straight up. For a minute I wondered if maybe I had raced all the way off the field and run into one of the light poles. I saw an M-80 go off, a pink snowfall, and then everything that was light went dark, and everything that was dark went light, exactly as if you were seeing a negative of the world.

I still wasn't right when I got back to the huddle; I hadn't even looked to see where the ball was put down.

"What'd I get, Ike?" I asked.

"Back to the line of scrimmage," he said.

All at once I was sore at Mel Edmonds, knowing he must have missed the crackback block, but when I finally found his face in the huddle, I saw that his nose was bleeding, so I let it go.

We ran the same play again, only this time I fed the ball to Stone and he made three yards.

Now it was third and seven, and we had to pass. I called a play where we throw to Foxx coming out of the backfield on a little delay, and I made sure we went to the opposite side, away from McClendon. Foxx nearly didn't catch the ball—it was thrown slightly behind him—but once he got control of it, he rambled. He was finally ganged out of bounds at the Baxter eighteen. Again the crowd went wild, and I mean *really* wild this time because Foxx was their boy. That was all right with me. What mattered was the fact that we had now moved the ball from our twenty to their eighteen in exactly four plays, Pete Stallings at the throttle.

Unfortunately, however, that's as far as we were going. We ran the option twice without making an inch— McClendon and his end had swapped assignments by this time, and when the pitch went to Foxx, he creamed Billy-boy the same way he'd creamed me. On third down a pass

121

intended for Skate was broken up in the end zone, so it was fourth and ten and we were still at their eighteen. I called time out and went over to talk to Dad.

"What do you think, Pete? A sprint-out? Something to Foxx?"

"I'm thinking field goal," I said.

"Huh?"

"Why not?"

"Skate can't kick it from there."

"No, but I can."

He looked at me, then took out a Chap-stick and ran it over his lips. "You think you can do it?"

"It would be nice to get on the board first," I said, "even if it's only three points. Give us a big psychological advantage."

"You're right," he said. "Go ahead and try it. They'd get the ball at the twenty anyway."

So we lined up, feeling strange doing something we'd never once practiced, and with Foxx holding, I drilled that baby through the uprights. It would have been good from another ten yards away.

As we came back up the field, the band was playing and of course the crowd was cheering, but my feelings were not all that optimistic. I had a sneaking hunch it might be a long, weary time before we got that close to Baxter's goal line again, and it would have been so much better if we could have made the touchdown. But then I remembered my positive thinking, and I gave myself a little pep talk. "What are you grousing about, Stallings? You've done something nobody's been able to do all year—you've moved the

122

ball all the way down for a score on Baxter without having to give it up. You've improvised; you've done the unexpected; you've kept them off balance. You've got them worried."

Unfortunately, I was right the first time.

On the kickoff I hit the ball good and put it all the way down to the goal line, and then made the tackle myself at the seventeen or eighteen with a little help from Hank Stern, our left tackle. (It's surprising how often that will happen, where the guy who kicks the ball is the one who gets the runner.) But from that point on, things got a little grim. After all, Baxter was a well-coached, confident football team accustomed to winning, and that piddling three-point lead of ours didn't exactly strike terror in their hearts. They went to work in a business-like manner, and when we finally brought them to a halt, they were inside our twenty. It was mostly routine power stuff—slants and sweeps and the belly series—but it was like trying to stop a Sherman tank by throwing yourself in front of it. Their quarterback was bigger than me—in fact, he was the largest man in their backfield—and though he wasn't supposed to be a particularly good passer, he was a first-rate ball handler, and on a roll-out or an option, a 195-pound quarterback is going to get you something, right? Usually about six yards. They also had a very fast black boy at tailback and a pulling guard that could make you hear birds and bells when he caught you right.

But we did stop them finally on a fourth-and-one situation at our nineteen, and the credit for that goes to Dave Stone, playing left-side linebacker. He and Ike both were playing super, but they were taking a beating.

We couldn't move at all, and I wasn't about to tempt fate with another pass that deep in our territory, so with fourth-and-five Stone dropped back to punt and sailed a beauty all the way up and out of bounds at midfield.

Then it started over again with the Baxter infantry marching through us like Sherman through Georgia. Only this time they started at the fifty and drove it down to our nine. All that saved us was another great effort by Ike and Dave.

We took over there, and on the first play of the series Foxx found daylight, running the ball back out to the twenty-one. But again we floundered and had to punt.

Same thing over again. Here they came, play after play like a herd of elephants, and by the middle of the second quarter they were lining up at our four-yard line with a third-and-one. It looked as if there was no way on earth we could stop them this trip. We of course called time out, drank some water, and held a little prayer meeting; but I doubt if there was a guy on the field that had any real hope of stopping them.

As it happened, Lady Luck came to our rescue. Or maybe that pause in the action threw their timing off. Anyway, on the third-down play they had a busted signal. Somebody ran into the quarterback instead of taking the handoff, and he dropped the ball. It bounced around all over the place back there for a while, and though they eventually got it back, all at once Baxter had a fourth-down situation, with *seven* to go instead of one.

Even that didn't seem to faze them—they had so much poise, it came close to arrogance. But when they tried the sweep, Ike and Billy Foxx and I were all three there to greet them, and they came up short of the first down by about a yard and a half.

So we had stopped them for the third time, and now it was our ball on our own five-yard line. I called the quarterback sneak, hoping to get it out a few yards so Stone would have room to kick; but when I walked up behind Ike, I saw McClendon right in front of me, grinning through that face cage. He had a way of reaching up, just before the snap, and pulling that cage down a little to set his helmet firmly on his head. It was an ominous gesture, something like a bull lowering his head and pawing the dirt. All at once I wished I had called some other play—any other play besides one where I had to carry the mail.

To make a short story even shorter, I didn't get anything except a fat lip, and on the next call Foxx didn't get anything either. So on third down we surprised them with Tennessee's old quick kick. It was a good, low boot, probably because he had to hurry to get it off, and to our surprise and relief it rolled all the way up near midfield again.

Baxter took over and cranked up the steamroller for the fourth time. I might add that they were getting a little irked by now, maybe even a little frustrated, at not being able to put a score on the board. I should also point out that all this strenuous activity on the gridiron had eaten up a sizable chunk of the clock. In describing the action, I'm trying to touch only the high spots, but during all this the usual things were going on—substitutions, first-down measurements, a couple of penalties, even a minor injury or two. Keep in mind also that Baxter is a very slow, deliberate team; they don't hurry anything until the ball is snapped.

126

What I'm trying to say is that when Baxter started their fourth big push of the ball game, there was only a minute and forty-five seconds left in the half. I felt that if we could go into the dressing room with a three-point edge, we might have enough of a psychological advantage to stay on top the rest of the way. I'll admit it was a pretty vain hope, especially when you took a look at the stats—they must have had a dozen first downs and no telling how many yards— but football games aren't decided by statistics. They are decided by what's on the scoreboard. Our guys had taken a terrific beating, that's true—particularly our linebackers and interior linemen. But that has to work both ways, and old Ike and Dave had dealt out some misery, too. When it came to physical conditioning, we were as good as anybody. So if we could only hold them . . .

We did better than that, as things turned out. You see, the clock was in our favor now. Baxter didn't want that first half to end with them still behind. So on the second play of the series they did something they hadn't done all night. They passed.

We play the zone, and when I saw their flanker come down and cut back through the middle toward the weak side, I didn't do a thing but hide. The quarterback was watching the end run a post, trying to get behind Foxx; but that wasn't in the cards, and then I saw him turn his head and hunt his flanker. I stayed hid—which is to say, instead of immediately coming up to cover the guy, I laid back a little, baiting him. This is a dangerous thing to do. Against a really good passer it's suicide, because what you're counting on is being able to get between the receiver and the ball

127

after it's thrown. But this time it worked. As soon as he released the ball, I knew it was mine. The pass was too soft —he sort of hung it out there—and the flanker, looking back over his right shoulder, had no idea there was anybody in the neighborhood. He was already wondering how far he could run after he caught it.

I'm the one who caught it. I took it on the dead run, which I'll admit is not exactly the speed of light, but by the time they realized what had happened, I had a start on everybody except the quarterback himself and the tailback who had stayed with him as a blocker. Suddenly Pete Stallings is going down the left sideline like the *Queen Mary* dragging a sea anchor. I'll tell you, though, fifty-five yards is a long way to run when you've already played two quarters of football. I saw I had the quarterback beaten, but not the tailback. He had the angle on me, and just when I was thinking he'll probably wipe me out around the twenty-five or thirty, something orange showed up at the corner of my eye. I took a quick look over my shoulder, and it was Mel Edmonds, coming up to try and help with a block— though how he got there, I still don't know to this day. Mel's fast, and he was gaining, but I knew he'd never get there in time.

Revelation number three.

Without even looking to see if *he* was looking, I tossed the ball back in the air to my right and threw a cross-body block into the tailback that sent him into the nickel seats.

I never saw it happen, but they told me later that Mel juggled the ball for fifteen yards before he finally found the handle—but he never stopped running. He went over the

128

goal line in a big looping arc and then threw that football so high in the air, it went clear out of the lights before it came back down.

The band played and the fans went ape.

When Skate kicked the point, the band played again and the fans continued ape.

We kicked off to them, and two plays later the half ended.

Score: Morgan County 10, Baxter zip.

13

"All right, all right, let's not get too excited!" Dad said, looking a good bit more excited than anybody else in the room. "We've had some breaks, we've played some great defensive football, and right now we're ten points ahead. But this ball game isn't over yet. It's only half over. Remember, last Friday night *we* were two touchdowns behind and still came back to win. We can't let up for a minute. They're beating us everywhere but on the scoreboard, but if we can hold what we've got, it's going to be a great night for Morgan County!"

He raved on like that for a while longer, telling us in one breath that we were doing great and in the next breath we might still get beat, until finally I wasn't sure whether it was a pep talk or a prophecy of disaster. Then Coach Dale got up and started making some adjustments on the interior line positions, and I let my mind drift off to other matters. How was everybody holding up physically, I wondered. Looking around the room, I saw that Dave Stone had a mouse under one eye, Mel Edmonds' nose was beginning to look like Jocko the Clown's, and Jake Grider was sitting with his hand against his ribs, taking little shallow swallows of air as if it hurt him to breathe. Andy Holmes, our middle guard, was getting a new splint taped to his thumb; he'd played the last four games with a broken thumb.

Then my eyes lit on Billy Foxx, and I saw a study in dejection. Foxx was sitting on the bench with his back against the wall, his elbows on his knees, and his head propped up on his hands. I knew he was pooped, but the look on his face told me more than that. He was like a little boy who has just dropped his ice cream on the sidewalk and sees the sun melting it away. The great climax runner had sure been an anticlimax tonight. Except for that one carry on the delay pass, he could have been running all evening on a dime and still had nine cents' change left over. For a minute I almost felt sorry for him—I have my weak moments—but then I reminded myself of all the games I'd played with his cheers in my ears, and that foolish emotion went away. They say every dog has his day, and this old dog was finally having his. I was playing a whale of a ball game and I knew it. Nobody had to tell me.

From that point I went off into a sort of reverie or daydream. The scene was the big banquet tomorrow night, and they were giving out the awards . . .

"Pete!"

"Yes, sir."

"Will you please pay attention to what I'm saying?"

"Sorry, Dad."

"The option has not worked, so I'm changing the blocking assignments. Instead of Edmonds on the crackback, I want

Skate hitting the rover, and Edmonds will go down on a pass route to draw the halfback away."

"Now you're talking, Coach-o," Skate said. "I'll climb that Godzilla like a monkey going up a coconut tree."

Everybody laughed, and I saw Grider clap a hand to his ribs and grimace.

"Pete, if the halfback doesn't go back with Edmonds, throw to him. Right?"

"Right."

He went on talking, but again my mind drifted off—I must have been still a little addled from that collision with McClendon. Out on the field the band was playing, and the half-time show was in progress. I could hear the part where they play the theme from *Exodus,* and for some loony reason I got to thinking how in three years of football games I had never seen the half-time show. We heard the music, through concrete walls, but for all I knew, the cheerleaders and majorettes could be dancing naked out there. Three years and thirty ball games, and I had never seen the half time. Just to show you how dopey I was, this thought began to prey on my mind, and I started to get sore about it. Was it so unreasonable to ask that once in a while the team be allowed to stay on the field and see the show? Weird.

Then I thought to myself, no, that's wrong because earlier this year I did get to see part of the show. It was at Homecoming when Patsy was runner-up for queen and I hurriedly changed into my Sunday suit and marched out with her at the presentation.

Patsy. Because I was having such a great game, my spirits were good, up to that point; but when I thought of Pat, it was like a cloud passing over my mind. Doggone it, I thought, why does there always have to be something to spoil it when things finally start going your way? If it wasn't for busting up with Pat, this would probably be the biggest night of my life. The same problem would be facing me tomorrow night, too, at the awards dinner and later at the dance. I'd be there stag, like some stupid jerk with dandruff or leprosy or something. Well, one thing: I wasn't going to show up stag. I'd think of somebody to drag, even if she was the ugliest girl in school.

That's how I spent the half time, thinking crazy stuff like that instead of listening to the coaches.

But soon we were back on the field, and the second half was ready to start. The ref blew his whistle and dropped his arm, and I was moving toward the ball there on the tee, feeling the eyes of several thousand people. Right then my head cleared and my concentration came back.

I hit it pretty good, high and deep, and watched it come down end over end into their quarterback's hands. He started to his right, and all the movement on the field swept that way, too, like colored leaves blown or sucked by a gust of wind—all but one guy, their tailback. I saw him going past the ball carrier, running against the grain, and though I couldn't actually see the exchange, I knew the quarterback had handed him the ball.

I yelled, "Reverse!" but the crowd was making such a racket, I don't think anybody heard me. Skate saw it, and Mel Edmonds, but both of them were cut down the instant they reversed their field. All at once he was outside everybody and coming up the right sideline with nobody to

134

worry about but me. It was that quick. As I moved to the right to head him off, I was thinking, "It's you or nobody, Petronovich. Don't let him get away." Somebody threw a block against the side of my left leg that came awful close to a clip, but I managed to fend him off and keep my feet. I was giving ground as the runner came up the field toward me, but at the same time I was pinching him in against the sideline. This boy was no slouch, let me tell you. He was built like Billy Foxx and plenty fast, and as the gap closed between us, he gave me a couple of hip fakes that would have looked good on a hula dancer. He wanted to break it back toward the middle, where he'd have room to maneuver, but that's exactly what I didn't mean to allow, and at the last minute he did a little two-step hesitation and turned on a burst of speed, trying to shoot through between me and the sideline. I mean I racked him. I put a cross-body block on him that had all of me in it and carried both of us into the Baxter bench, bowling over several players and some guy in a parka that was either a coach or a trainer.

Well, it looked good and it saved us a touchdown, but in the final analysis I guess it wasn't all that big a deal. All it really accomplished was a delay.

Baxter cranked up their steamroller again, and nine plays later they punched it over from the two with the same kid hauling the leather.

They kicked the point, and with less than six minutes gone in the third quarter, they had narrowed our margin from ten points to three.

We talked it up big in the huddle, and for the next few exchanges everybody, including Billy Foxx, really gave it a good hustle. We made a couple of first downs but never actually threatened, and then just before the end of the third quarter, Baxter scored again on a sweep that sent Jake Grider out of the game with a fractured rib.

Gloom settled over the east stands. We were behind for the first time, 14 to 10, and we were now playing them with two of our regular starters out of the game—Teas and Grider. Not only that, this guy McClendon seemed to be getting stronger as the night wore on. At first when we ran the option, he stopped us; now when we tried it, he was throwing us for losses. It didn't make any difference whether I gave the ball to Stone, kept it myself, or pitched it to Foxx, McClendon arrived early and emphatic. He was brutal—there's no other word for it. Gradually as the minutes of the last quarter ticked away, I could see some of our guys beginning to give up—no, not giving up exactly, but beginning to see the handwriting on the wall. We were behind and we simply could not move the ball, and I guess in their minds that added up to defeat, especially now that time was running out. None of us knew it then, but the worst was yet to come.

With a little more than six minutes left in the game, Baxter completed a couple of passes that took them down to our twenty-eight, and then on a third-and-short situation they surprised us with another pass that was complete at the three. We held them for three downs—probably our finest defensive effort of the whole game—but on fourth down their fullback wedged over for the score.

For some reason they decided to go for two, throwing to the wingback on what we call a quick out, but I managed to get a hand on the ball and batted it down.

136

When we lined up to receive the kickoff, there were four minutes left in the game and the score was 20 to 10 in their favor. Glancing up at the stands, I saw a trickle of people starting down the aisles—faint-hearted fans who had already thrown in the towel and were now thinking of getting out of the parking lot before the big traffic jam.

This time the ball fell to me at the ten, and I staggered out to the twenty-seven before they derailed me. (Derailed is a good word because when these guys start colliding with you, it is like trying to survive a train wreck.) On the first play of the series I ran the roll-out and got slaughtered, and on second down I ran the same play and got slaughtered again. But I was setting them up for something.

On the third down I called a play that starts like the roll-out, but instead I throw a pass to Skate running a deep flag pattern—in other words, the "bomb." It's hard to throw long when you're running; you need to set your feet for that kind of pass. But I was a desperate man, and I guess the old Adrenalin came to my aid, giving me that extra Wheatie I needed to get it down there. Actually, I released the ball before Skate ever looked back. He was running hard, straight at their halfback, and all I could do was guess at the distance. I made sure it was long enough to go over the defensive man's head, but I threw it a little to the left of where it should have gone. A flag pattern means the receiver goes straight down the field, then cuts toward the red flag at the corner of the end zone, and if he's running it to the right, he naturally looks back for the ball over his right shoulder.

As soon as Skate had his man beaten, he looked back,

saw the ball was behind him, then turned his head and caught it over his left shoulder, all in one motion. It was truly a thing of beauty. He was going so fast when he crossed the goal line that he ran all the way across the track and into the fence.

The crowd roared to life again, the band struck up the "Stars and Stripes Forever," and after Skate got his breath and kicked the extra point, we came back up the field to a hero's welcome. We were in the ball game again, only three points behind. Suddenly I was feeling great, trembling on the verge of another one of my famous revelations. But then I remembered the clock, and when I looked, my heart sank. There was less than three minutes' playing time left, and Baxter would now have the football. It would be hard to ever get it back from them in that short a time.

I went to the sidelines for a confab with Dad and Coach Dale and came away with instructions to try an on-sides kick.

Foxx laid the ball on its laces, and I squibbed it off to the left. Our guys were down there fast, but a big Baxter tackle fell on it hard enough to bust it.

The kick hadn't worked; they were in business at their own forty-five, and the ref was running to both huddles to announce the two-minute warning. Now our only hope of getting our hands on the ball again before the game ended was to pray for a fumble, or do something we hadn't been able to do all night—hold them for three, possibly four downs.

Believe it or not, we did. We were really fired up by this time, and on a fourth-and-one near midfield, Baxter went into punt formation. At first I didn't believe it; but then when I looked back over my shoulder at the clock, it made more sense. There was less than a minute left in the game. Baxter was willing for us to have the ball deep in our own territory, but they couldn't risk our getting it out here at midfield where another desperation pass might beat them.

As Foxx went back into deep safety, I ran over and grabbed his arm.

"Get out of bounds with it," I said. "Whatever you do, don't let them tackle you in bounds, you hear me? We've got only one time-out left." I was thinking two, possibly three pass plays were left to us if we could get that clock stopped.

Foxx looked at me, blank as a goose, and trotted on down the field.

It was a good, booming high kick toward the corner— one of those tantalizers that makes you wonder how to play it. With a straight-ahead bounce it would go into the end zone, giving us first-and-ten at the twenty. But if it kicked to the right, it would go out of bounds around the five, leaving us in a desperate hole.

I needn't have worried because Foxx evidently had no intention of letting it bounce in any direction. He streaked back to his left, caught the ball over his shoulder, and circled at least three yards deep in the end zone before he got turned around and headed back up the field.

Well, when he came, he came, mister. For the first time all night long we saw Billy Foxx doing what Billy Foxx does best. He shagged, he faked, he sidestepped, he spun away from tackle after tackle, right up the middle of the field through the whole Baxter team. Remember what I said

139

back at the start of this about the climax runners? Well, here it was in its purest form, and I got so fascinated watching him that I almost forgot to knock anybody down—almost but not quite. I folded their right end and then just sort of wallowed around on him to make sure he didn't get up again too quickly.

They finally brought Foxx down at the Baxter twelve—an eighty-eight-yard miracle that had the crowd in hysterics.

We lined up without a huddle, and I threw the ball over Edmonds' head and out of bounds to stop the clock. Nobody heard my "hike!"—you couldn't have heard a cannon shot in that stadium with the racket the crowd was making — and two or three people jumped off sides for both teams. The refs held a pow-wow, decided on nullifying penalties, and we huddled again with the ball still spotted at the twelve. There were twelve seconds on the clock.

"I'm sorry I didn't get out of bounds, Pete," Foxx said in the huddle. He was breathing so hard that he could hardly talk.

I reached over, grabbed his face guard, and gave it a shake. "The guy's apologizing for eighty-eight yards!"

The ball was spotted at the left hash mark, so I called the roll-out, ran to my right until I was directly in front of the goalposts, and then cut upfield into the waiting arms of you-know-who. He hit me so hard that I saw those lights again, only this time they were target-shaped rings that started in the middle of my head and expanded. But I did manage to scramble to my feet and make the T sign with my hands.

It's a good thing we had one more time-out left because at that moment I was in no condition to continue the ball game. When I finally got my eyes in focus, I saw two things almost simultaneously: a fuzzy eight seconds on the clock and Dad coming out on the edge of the field to meet me.

I shook my head and waved him back.

He stood there looking dumbfounded for a second, but then suddenly he grinned, gave me the old V-for-victory with two fingers, and turned back toward the bench.

I went back to where the guys were resting on the grass in a big loose circle. They were panting and wheezing and mopping sweat, and nobody was saying a word, not even Skate. I pulled my helmet off and dropped to one knee in the middle of the circle.

"Well, guys," I said, "this is it."

Not a very original statement, I must admit, but it summed up the situation better than anything else I could think of. There was time for one more play—two if we were lucky, but I didn't want to count on it. One more play to decide the football game. All that sweat and strain and agony that had been going on for four quarters, and now it boiled down to a single play, who would win, who would lose. Right then I had one of my crazy notions: it didn't seem fair for *either* team to lose this game.

Billy Foxx must have been thinking the same thing because he spoke up then and said: "You can do it, Pete. You kicked one farther back than this in the first quarter."

"Yeah," said Ike Mathis. "And we've got better position this time, right in front of the goalposts."

When it dawned on me what they were thinking, I went sort of cold all over, and then I started to get mad.

"You mean kick a field goal? Go for the *tie?*"

Practically every one of them looked up at me in surprise.

"Sure," said Edmonds. "We've got it locked. A tie is like a moral victory against this bunch. Besides, we haven't made twelve yards the whole second half, except on something wild. We might as well be camped at the fifty if you don't kick the field goal."

All at once I was really steaming. "Wait just a minute," I said. "Are you that same Mel Edmonds Dad was talking about in the dressing room before the game? I mean the guy he wishes we all had his kind of guts?"

Mel hung his head a little at that.

Then I turned on Foxx. "Yeah, and what's wrong with you tonight, glamour-boy? You ready to hang up the strap, too? That big punt return will get your picture in the paper no matter how the game turns out—is that all that matters to you?"

He opened his mouth to say something, but I didn't let him.

"What the hell is this, the give-up boys of '72? What's happened to your guts?"

Nobody said anything.

"Listen. We may not win this ball game, but we sure as hell aren't going to settle for a tie. Not as long as I'm calling the plays. I didn't come out here to compromise; I came to win!"

"You tell 'em, big daddy!" Skate said. "What I got these bruises for—break even? Man, we was *even* before we started this mess!"

Skate, as usual, hit exactly the right lick. Everybody broke up laughing (which must have sounded a little crazy

143

to the Baxter team over there), and in an instant the whole mood was changed. You could feel it happening, like a fresh charge of electricity running around that circle.

"All right, so we go for broke," Stone said. "There may be time for two passes if we miss the first one. I think you ought to call both plays now so we don't have to waste time with a huddle after the first one."

I was already shaking my head. "Pass won't get it, Dave. They'll be looking for that."

"What, then?"

"Well, who's our best running back?"

There was a moment of hesitation, everybody swapping glances, then Ike spoke up and said, "Foxx."

"And what's been our best play all season?"

"Now wait a minute," Foxx said. "Pete, they've killed us all night on the option. You must be out of your mind."

"Well, it's not going to be exactly an option this time," I said. "It's going to be a pitch back to you."

"But . . ."

"Listen quick now—we're about out of time. We'll start the play to the right just like the option, but you'll lag a little more than usual. Mel, you go down to decoy the halfback. Skate, can you take care of the end?"

"I'll make him wish he was back picking cotton. Hey, but wait a minute. Who gets Godzilla?"

"Me."

"*You?*" said Foxx. "How on earth can you do that?"

"He'll be coming. That's why I want you to lag . . . so I'll have time to get him in my sights after I throw you the ball."

144

There was total silence—skeptical silence. Finally Dave Stone broke it. "You really think this'll work, Pete?"

"I don't know, Dave. But at least it's something we haven't tried before. I'm willing to give it a shot if the rest of you are."

The whistle sounded, and there was a rousing shout as we scrambled to our feet, pulled on our helmets, and fastened up the chin straps. We made a quick huddle, but all I said to them was this: "All right, gang, this one is for Jack Teas!"

There was a sharp clap as we broke the huddle and ran up to the line, and six or seven thousand people came to their feet in a single motion. Across the line I saw McClendon drift to his left as we formed strong to our right. He was bending slightly from the waist, those long arms hanging loose and relaxed, loving every moment of it. I had to admire this guy, like him or not. But then I saw his hand come up and give that face cage a tug, and I stopped thinking foolish thoughts.

"Readeeee, hike!"

The ball smacked my hands; I stepped back and pivoted to the right. As I started moving, I could see Foxx in the corner of my eye, matching me stride for stride like my own shadow. Mel had already fired off the line and was almost to the end zone when Skate drove his shoulder into the end to open that gap I was looking for outside the tackle. I didn't bother to look back, I just tossed the ball toward that shadow that was trailing me, and sure enough, here came McClendon like an express train. I knew I could never check him, much less knock him back. If I hit him high, he would simply jam the play by force. So I went down low and threw my hip at his knees. At the last instant he tried to hurdle me, but he didn't quite make it. The mighty oak of the forest crashed down on his face right across my butt . . . and two seconds later Billy Foxx flashed over the goal line standing up.

14

How do you describe pandemonium? Six thousand people going ape? No, make that only about four thousand going ape; there were a couple of thousand Baxter fans in the west stands that didn't exactly join the festivities. (By the way, Skate kicked the extra point and the game ended 24 to 20.) But otherwise, straight pandemonium. People were tearing their programs up in little pieces and throwing them in the air like confetti, the band was racing through everything it knew in double time, and several hundred fans even scaled the chain-link fence and came out on the field to congratulate us. They got Billy Foxx up on their shoulders and marched him around, holding him for other people who were shooting off photoflash bulbs in his face. That was OK, too. Tonight I wasn't going to be sore at anybody or jealous of anybody, not even . . .

"Pete?"

I turned, jostled and pushed by the crowd, and there · stood Patsy, smiling at me with tears streaming down both cheeks.

"Oh, hi, Pat."

"I just wanted to tell you I think you played the greatest game ever! Just super, Pete! I'm so proud of you I could cry."

I started to say, "Well, you already are crying," but somehow nothing came out.

She looked at me helplessly for a minute, still smiling that odd little broken-wing smile; then she raised her arms and let them fall against her sides, like "What's the use," and before I could reach out to stop her or even say thanks, she was gone again in the crowd.

"Pete!"

This time it was Jack Teas, also with tears in his eyes and all choked up with emotion.

"Doggone, you son of a gun, you did it! You did it!"

He threw his arms around me and swung on me as if I were a Maypole, dancing me around and around till we crashed into some other people, and then he was gone, too, rushing off to congratulate some other member of the team.

I had worked my way through the back-slappers to the edge of the field and was making a beeline toward the dressing room when all at once I saw a familiar figure moving across to head me off. It was McClendon. Sweaty, dirty —dragging, buddy. For an instant it flashed in my mind that this character might be sore about losing; maybe he was coming over for a little post-season head-knocking. I approached him, shall we say, warily.

"Stallings!" he foghorned.

"Yeah?"

Just before he came up to me, he pulled his helmet off,

and I saw his face, really saw it, for the first time. You could have knocked me over with a feather. I guess I was expecting some guy with a beard and fangs—I don't know. But what I saw was the freckled face of a seventeen-year-old kid, bruised and dusty . . . and streaked with tears. *Why is everybody crying,* I wondered. *Do we cry whether we lose or we win?*

He managed to smile, though, and that was funny, too, because he had big spaces between his teeth that made him look even younger than he was.

"Great game, Stallings," he said. "Congratulations. I was proud of you when you went for it instead of kicking a crappy little old field goal."

"Well, gee, thanks, Godz—I mean, Mac!"

"Coach told us you were the one we'd have to beat, and he was right."

Can you imagine that? Coach told them *I* was the one they'd have to beat?

I grabbed his big paw in both of mine and shook it. "Don't feel bad," I said. "I never spent a more miserable evening in my life."

His grin broadened. "I bust you pretty good?"

"Only God and my dentist will ever know."

That cheered him up a lot. He threw one of those big meat hooks around my shoulder and pulled me against him like a rag doll in a bear hug. "Take it easy, hear? Ya'll come."

I think he really meant it.

In the dressing room it was more of the same: pandemonium. Skate, stripped to the waist, was standing on one

150

of the benches leading cheers, and somebody in the shower stall was twisting one of the nozzles around to spray the whole room periodically. Dad came straight to me through the crowd and shook my hand without a word, and somehow that got to me so hard that damned if *I* didn't start to cry. I mean, it was an emotional moment, and of course we were all dead beat and completely sapped of anything you can use to hold back your emotions.

But what I did was get dressed as quickly as possible and ducked out of there.

In the corridor one of the trainers was sitting at a card table, passing out the little slips of paper for us to cast our vote for Most Valuable Player. I wrote "Foxx" on one, signed it, and dropped it in the cigar box.

Then I was out of there and in my jeep, headed for home.

The house was dark when I got there—Mom always waited to ride home with Dad—so I went up to my room, put a stack of Aretha Franklins on the stereo, and turned it way down low. Then I stretched out on my bed in the dark. I know it sounds goony, but it's exactly what I felt like doing. What I wanted more than anything was to be alone for a little while in a place where it was quiet and dark. I wasn't feeling anything much, except relief. Release.

It must have been nearly an hour before I heard the folks come home. I heard them in the carport, then heard them in the kitchen while Mom was putting on some of that famous coffee of hers. After a while Dad went in the study and closed the door, and a creak on the stairs told me Mom was coming up.

"Pete, can I come in?"

"Sure, Mom."

She didn't turn on the light, but left the door open so she could see me by the light from the hall. She came over to the bed, sat down, and ran her fingers through my hair, combing it back from my eyes. "You played a magnificent game, Pete. Your father's very proud of you."

"Yeah, it was a great victory for the team. But you know, it's funny—I don't feel anything."

"Can't you guess why?"

"Not exactly."

"It's because your happiness isn't complete. In fact, if I had to make a guess right now, I'd say you're probably sort of suspended between happiness and unhappiness. Why don't you give Patsy a call?"

"You think that's it?"

"I know it is, you dope. Us women have an unerring instinct in these matters—you said so yourself."

"She's probably out with Foxx by now."

"I happen to know she isn't."

"How would you know something like that?"

"Because I happened to sit with the Lloyds at the game tonight. I know a lot of things now that I didn't know yesterday."

"Like what, for instance?"

"Like why Billy Foxx went to see Patsy last Sunday afternoon."

"I hope you aren't going to tell me it was because he was having trouble with his Spanish. We've been through the rest of the curriculum."

She laughed that gay little laugh of hers and took my hand, lacing her fingers in mine the way I sometimes hold

152

hands with Patsy. "No, it was because he was having trouble with a friend of his—somebody he liked very much, whose friendship he valued, and who was acting coldly toward him. He was looking for an ally, somebody who might be able to tell him what was wrong and what he could do about it."

I sat up and tried to see her face in the dark. "Are you telling me the truth?"

"As I earnestly believe it."

"Then why didn't she just tell me that? Why all that rigmarole about Grandmother's house and trigonometry?"

"Well, it seems Billy made her promise *not* to tell you."

I shook my head and lay back down. "That's a little thin, Mom. I'm not sure I can buy that part. Isn't Billy taking her to the dance?"

"Nope. Patsy isn't going to the dance. She's had two invitations—neither of which were from Billy Foxx, I hasten to add—but she won't be there, Pete, unless you take her."

I lay there thinking about it, wanting to believe it, but something held me back.

"You're scared," Mom said, reading my mind. "She hurt you once and you're afraid she'll do it again. Right? You're chicken."

"Aw, Mom . . ."

"I'm going to say one more thing to you, Pete Stallings, and then I'm going to butt out. Are you ready to hear it?"

"Shoot."

"For a guy who doesn't know how to give up in a football game, you sure give up easy in the game of love. And you know something? That's the most fun game of all!"

She got all the way to the door before I stopped her.

"Mom, you suppose it's too late for me to go over there tonight?"

"It's never too late, Pete. You proved that against Baxter."

"No, I mean the old drop-kicker. He throws me out at the stroke of twelve, and it's almost midnight now."

She laughed again—having won her own little game for the night. "Somehow I have a hunch it'll be all right this time."

I got my shoes on, grabbed a coat, and beat it back downstairs. But as I started through the hall, I saw the light under the study door, and I stopped again. "Why not get it over with now?" I thought. "Why keep yourself hanging?"

"Dad?"

"Yes, son, come in."

He was propped back in his swivel chair, just lighting his pipe. The cigar box was there, and the ballots were spread out on the desk in front of him.

"By the way," I said very casually, "who got the award?" It took all the guts I could muster.

"Billy Foxx."

I don't know why it came so hard; subconsciously I'd known it all the time. Still the bitterness rose up in my throat—not at Foxx anymore, but at people in general . . . at life, fate, injustice . . . whatever you want to call it.

"Tell me something, Dad. Do you really think he played a better game out there tonight than I did?"

154

He shook his head. "You know he didn't, Pete. It was your block on McClendon that won it for us."

"Is he a better man out there than I am?"

"Are we a better football team than Baxter? Sure, we beat them tonight, but if we had to play them every night for a week—what about that?"

There wasn't much I could say, was there?

"Let's put it this way, Pete. Billy's a more stylish player than you are. He has a great love of the game and a terrific ability to come through with the big play when the chips are down—like that punt return tonight. *Someday* he'll be a much finer player than you are. Someday Billy Foxx will be a great college star, I firmly believe it. Another thing you've got to realize is this: he's the kind of player the crowd loves to watch. He gives them thrills, and after all, that's what they pay their money for."

"I see," I said. "I really don't feel too bad about not winning—it's just you, Dad. I know how badly you wanted me to take that cup, and . . . well, I hate to disappoint you."

"I'm not disappointed, Pete," he said quietly. "You played as fine a football game tonight as I ever saw a high school boy play. We have our moments, and you certainly achieved one of yours tonight. But more important, when the time came, you were able to make an unselfish decision and forget about yourself in the bigger interest of the team and the school. You see, that's what had me worried—not the cup. For a while after Billy Foxx came along, you weren't shaping up like the man I wanted you to be. Trophies only tell us what the rest of the world thinks of us,

155

Pete. What we really are is sometimes an entirely different matter."

All at once I felt a lot better. I felt like somebody had lifted a ten-ton load off my back.

"Dad," I said. "How many votes *did* I get?"

"You only got five, Pete. That's not many, is it? Out of fifty-two?"

"Mind telling me who they were?"

"No, I guess there's no harm in that. Fellow has a right to know his friends. You got Skate's vote of course, and Dave Stone, and Jack Teas. You also got Billy Foxx's vote, if that means anything to you."

"It sure does. In a way, it means more than any of them. I owe that guy a whole mess of apologies."

"Well, if you hurry, you might find him down around the Cave somewhere."

"Right. But first I have to pick up Patsy."

I was halfway down the hall before it struck me that there was something wrong with that count. I went back and stood in the doorway again, looking at him.

"Dad, I got five votes. Right?"

"That's right."

"But Skate and Stone and Teas and Foxx—that only adds up to four."

He looked up at me, and pride was shining in his eyes. "You got my vote, too, son," he said.

You know something? When I left the house that night to pick up Pat, I felt better than if I had won that doggone cup.

156